MW00982215

Magnus the Magnificent

Excerpts from "To Hope." John Keats, 1815, are unaccredited (p. 116, 121, 128).
ISBN: 1537005936
EAN-13: 978-1537005935
Cover photo: Andrew Fletcher/Shutterstock.com
Cover design: Kimberly Manky/Bria Carlson

Magnus the Magnificent

By Kimberly Manky

For Rhys,

who always tells me that I can.

Magnus

the

Magnificent

To Hope.

Whene'er the fate of those I hold most dear
Tells to my fearful breast a tale of sorrow,
O bright-eyed Hope, my morbid fancy cheer;
Let me awhile thy sweetest comforts borrow:
Thy heaven-born radiance around me shed,
And wave thy silver pinions o'er my head!

Should e'er unhappy love my bosom pain,
From cruel parents, or relentless fair;
O let me think it is not quite in vain
To sigh out sonnets to the midnight air!
Sweet Hope, ethereal balm upon me shed,
And wave thy silver pinions o'er my head!

- John Keats

Chapter 1

On November 13, 1942 a beautiful baby boy was born on the floor of a cold and cramped kitchenette in a caravan in East Anglia.

The father thought him to be a strapping young lad, his genitals swollen from the hormone increase after birth. Days later, the father caught a glimpse of his son in the bath. He couldn't hide his disappointment.

The disappointment extended beyond his circumstances. He was a frustrated, addled, and restless man. He was also a man that wouldn't be bound by obligation.

One afternoon he said he was going out for tobacco… He never returned.

The mother was left all alone with the new babe.

Birth takes its toll on a woman. A joyful woman can become instantly troubled, and the world can feel very heavy.

The mother soon became overwhelmed, and then listless; her spirit deflated like a punctured helium balloon.

When she looked at her son, she only saw the burden.

And the boy?

He did as children do. He got taller, and stronger, and smarter.

He grew up into a very charming young man, who was very fond of engaging in conversation with adults.

His mother encouraged this behavior as it left her alone with her thoughts.

The boy's name was Latin in origin, meaning "great," "large," or "swollen." His name was…

"Magnus."

I remember the day he was born. He had a full head of flaxen hair, and those bright, blue eyes.
Those eyes!
They were so full of life, and zest, and oomph.
O bright-eyed hope!

"Magnus?"

"Yes, Mum?" Magnus turned toward Mum, a middle-aged woman with downcast eyes and prematurely graying hair.

Mum spent her time knitting, reading political magazines, and rocking in her chair.

"Hurry on." Mum nodded her head toward the door.

Magnus moved to the window and wiped the condensation from the glass. "But it's raining very hard."

"Take a brolly and go."

Magnus started toward the front door, looking back at Mum every few steps. He pulled his heavy coat off the hook.

"Okay. Here I go." Magnus slipped into his wellies, and lifted an umbrella from the stand. "I'm off then."

Magnus looked over to the sideboard, where there stood a small souvenir clock shaped like the famous clock tower Big Ben. "I'll be home by five." Magnus stood, waiting for a response.

Without a word, Mum stood up from her chair, and wandered into the kitchenette.

She was still in her dressing gown.

Magnus opened the door to the blustery storm, and then turned back to declare his heart.

"I love you."

There was no response.

There never was... but that didn't stop Magnus from saying it.

You see, sometimes someone is so full of love that they can't help themselves, even when the person they adore can't, or won't, receive it.

Why can't they receive it?

Only they know.

Perhaps they were once hurt by someone they loved, and they were never able to forget.

Perhaps they've never really known what *love* is.

Or perhaps they have long forgotten what love feels like, so they wouldn't recognize it, even if it were standing right in front of them.

Magnus closed the door tightly behind him, and then checked to make sure it had latched.

"Did you say you loved your mum?"

Magnus turned around to find two toughs from school, Sam and Andy, walking past the caravan.

Magnus cleared his throat. "I do indeed. She's a wonderful woman with many wonderful qualities."

The boys just stared at Magnus.

"Where are you off to?" Andy shouted in Magnus' direction.

"The High Street." Magnus replied, as he carefully stepped down the stairs to the caravan.

"Us too. Shall we all walk together then?"

Magnus could hardly contain his excitement. "Yes, please!" Magnus ran to catch up to the boys, grinning from ear to ear.

The boys walked in silence for a few paces, and then Magnus piped up. "I didn't think you liked me."

"Whatever would make you think that?" Andy asked, nudging Sam in the ribs.

"Because you say unkind things to me, you never want to play with me, and sometimes you play games where I don't exist."

Andy suddenly turned toward Magnus. "Do you collect stamps?"

Magnus smiled. "Yes, I do have a small collection."

"Well then, here's one for ya!" Andy lifted his leg up and brought it down hard on Magnus' foot.

Magnus squealed with pain, hopping up and down on one foot.

Andy laughed. "Look at him. Mother's little darling sissy."

Sam turned and gave Magnus a shove, sending him tumbling into the shallow ditch.

Andy shook his head. "You didn't think we really wanted to be pals, did ya?"

Magnus' lower lip began to quiver. He pressed his finger to his lip to prevent the movement.

Sam pointed at Magnus. "Cry, baby, cry."

"Come on!" Andy grabbed Sam's arm and the two of them ran off, leaving Magnus with his buttocks and boots firmly entrenched in the sludge.

Children can be so cruel.

Magnus slowly rose to his feet and pulled a pristine, white handkerchief from his coat pocket. He looked over to the nearby pasture, where several dozen sheep were grazing.

A little lamb suckled at its mother's teat.

The mother.

The lamb.

As he began wiping the mud from his trousers, the sun broke through the clouds and the rain ceased.

Chapter 2

T he doorbell chimed as Magnus stepped inside the butcher's shop.
The shop was bright, with white tiles on the wall, sawdust on the
floor, and a large side of beef hanging from a hook in the ceiling.

The butcher stood at the counter making sausages. He was a
very large man with a flushed face and thick, short fingers.

Magnus watched as the butcher pulled the long, limpid wursts
from the machine and checked their casings.

"Good afternoon, sir." Magnus stood up on his tippy-toes to
look over the high counter.

"Aye."

"Mum wanted me to inform you that your flank steak was
delicious. She said she's never eaten a more succulent cut of beef in
her entire life, and considering she's in her early forties, that's saying

quite a lot." Magnus paused briefly, before continuing: "And she asked me to send her best to you and your wife."

The butcher wiped his hands on his bloodied apron, and looked down at Magnus. "I'm not sure I've ever met your mum."

Magnus raised his eyebrows. "No?"

"Come to think of it, I've only ever seen you in here on your own."

Magnus smiled. "Well, to be completely honest, Mum is a very sociable woman so it's hard to keep tabs. I'm sure she meant it only as a friendly form of discourse, and not as a literal greeting."

The butcher tilted his head, and then leaned on the counter. "So what'll it be?"

Magnus pointed at the sausages. "What have you got there?"

"Lamb with rosemary."

Magnus looked pained, and placed his hand over his heart. "I don't eat lamb… For sentimental reasons."

The butcher rolled his eyes.

"Quarter pound of suet, please."

Magnus scanned the case, as the butcher ripped the paper from the roll and began packing it up.

"Thank you very much, kind sir." Magnus took the package and handed the butcher two coins. "And you have yourself a wonderful day!"

"And you." The butcher sent Magnus off with a nod.

As Magnus exited the butcher's shop, a young woman pushing a pram waved from across the road. "Good afternoon, Magnus."

"Good afternoon, Mrs. Chapman!" Magnus called as he waved in her direction.

Magnus stopped in front of the Greengrocers, and looked at his reflection in the windowpane. His trousers were filthy and his hair was mussed. As he pulled out a small comb to smooth his hair, Magnus peered through the window to see a crate of beautiful, ripe, clingstone peaches.

Magnus stepped inside the store, which was crowded with shelves upon shelves of dry and tinned goods, and fresh produce propped up in the front window.

Magnus made his way over to the crate, and picked up a small, perfect peach. He held it up to his nose, inhaling the fruit's essence. He closed his eyes, and touched the fruit's skin to his cheek.

"Excuse me! What do you think you're doing?"

Magnus' eyes popped open to see a stock boy with one, excessive, furrowed brow.

"Those peaches are not to be handled! They've been brought in by special request for the holidays."

"I'm sorry... I fell into a bit of a daydream. The aroma of these lovely peaches took me right back to when I was a small boy living in Athens."

The stock boy looked around the store. "Does your mum know that you're out on your own?"

Magnus wrinkled his nose. "Do you think that I am some sort of helpless vagrant? I'm ten years old for heaven's sake. Turning eleven next November, thank you very much."

"You're turning eleven *next* November?"

"Yes."

"Well, it's just December..." The stock boy placed his hands firmly on his hips. "So you're just ten."

"True."

"You're going to need to purchase that peach."

Magnus smiled. "It would be my absolute pleasure to purchase this 'prunis persica.'"

The stock boy looked at him blankly.

Magnus smiled. "It's Latin... For peach."

"Do you have money to pay for this?" The stock boy asked, as he led Magnus to the counter.

"Of course. I come from a family with money." Magnus paused, and looked up at the stock boy. "Old money. Please don't hate me because of my circumstance."

How shall I say this delicately?
Dear Magnus was a teller of untruths...
Magnus did not grow up in Athens, or come from a family with "old" money. And that was certainly not the first tall tale that he had told.
Because sometimes, spinning a yarn is easier than telling the truth.

As the stock boy pushed Magnus toward the counter, he noticed Magnus' trousers. "If you're so well-heeled, why do your trousers have holes?"

Magnus looked down at the holes and rips.

"Well?" The stock boy prodded.

Magnus smiled. "Because I'm a ten year-old boy with a keen sense of adventure."

The Stock Boy stood with arms crossed.

"And sometimes my clothes pay the price."

Chapter 3

The table was set for two.

"Tea's ready," Magnus called.

There was no response.

The kitchenette of the caravan was cramped, with a small table and two narrow benches crowding most of the galley.

Magnus' legs dangled from the bench, as he spread jam on his toast and stared out the small, paned window to the neighboring field, which was dusted with frost.

"Mum? Tea's ready."

Magnus placed his knife carefully down on the plate, and stood up. He pushed open the flap door to the living area and saw Mum slouched on the settee, fast asleep, with a delicate smile on her lips.

Magnus moved closer, side-stepping the balls of yarn and political magazines that were scattered across the carrot-colored carpet.

Magnus stared down at Mum.

The years had taken their toll, but she had no wrinkles to speak of... No lines to define where she had ever smiled, or laughed, or squinted her eyes at the sun.

Magnus picked up the striped woolen blanket from the floor, and gently laid it over her slight frame.

Chapter 4

The rooster crowed at 8:02am.

Magnus' eyes popped open and his gaze shifted to the water stains on the ceiling. The sepia stains looked like continents drifting slowly apart.

He inhaled sharply, and rolled out of bed.

Magnus wiped the frost from the window. The sun was just peeking over the hills to the East, illuminating the sheep huddled together in the snowy pasture.

There was a knock at the door. "Magnus, you up?"

"Yes, Mum." Magnus pulled open the closet door and quickly dressed, tugging on his school uniform of gray shorts and long gray socks.

Magnus was still buttoning his shirt as he made his way to the kitchenette.

"Good morning." Magnus declared as he entered the room. "You're up early."

Mum sat at the table, warming her hands around her teacup, and staring vacantly out the window. "Hurry on. You're going to be late."

Magnus nodded, as he pulled a piece of bread from the canister.

…

Magnus' school was a three-story rusted red brick slab, with very few windows and a large rectangular clock face in the middle of its façade.

He climbed the steps quickly and slipped inside. Children lined both sides of the corridor, giggling, pointing, and whispering as Magnus made his way past.

Andy thumbed his nose at Magnus, and Magnus pretended not to notice.

Magnus stopped at Room 108. The door was open a crack, and Magnus pushed it open as he entered. The classroom was dim, and cold. The black, pot-bellied stove crackled in the corner, as it began to warm the room.

Magnus proceeded to a desk in the front row. He sat down and folded his hands neatly in front of him.

And he tried very hard not to cry.

The bell rang, and the lights snapped on, illuminating the children as they pushed into the classroom. Their faces were flushed and their hair was damp from the wintry English morning.

Magnus' Teacher entered. She was a rakish woman of 60, with thin wrists and even thinner ankles. All of which looked as though they might snap with the slightest bend.

The children only knew her as "Teacher," not miss or missus.

"Sit children!" Teacher pounded her slight fist on her desk. The children immediately hushed. "Right to work on your maths. Page 30. Single-spaced. Without a word!" There was a quiet shuffle as the children took out their books. "I said without a word!"

As Magnus opened his textbook, a paper aeroplane floated in his direction, landing on the corner of his desk. A smile spread over Magnus' lips, and he turned to look in the direction of its launch. All of the children had their heads buried in their books.

"Excuse me, Teacher?" Andy piped up.

Magnus looked back at Andy, his hand sticking straight up in the air.

Teacher did not look amused. "Yes, Andy?"

"Magnus is playing with a paper aeroplane. I fear it might become a distraction."

"Is that so?" Teacher's chair screeched as she stood up. She marched over to Magnus' desk, snatching the paper aeroplane off his desk. "Is this yours?"

"No," Magnus replied anxiously.

"Well then, to whom does it belong?" Teacher held the aeroplane up in the air for all to see.

"I don't know." Magnus lowered his head.

Teacher leaned hard on Magnus' desk, her brittle wrists on the verge of collapse. "I asked you once, and I will only ask you once more. Where did it come from?"

Magnus looked around the room. All of the children avoided his gaze. "I don't know."

"Well then, what *do* you know?" Teacher crumpled the aeroplane up into a ball, and dropped it in the rubbish bin. "Perhaps you can think about what you *do* know whilst sitting on the bench at lunch." Teacher moved swiftly back to her desk, and picked up a pad of paper and a *very* sharp pencil. "In fact, you will spend your lunch break writing down every single thing that you *do* know."

Teacher walked over to Magnus' desk and set the pad and pencil on the corner. "Anyone else keen to become a distraction?"

The room became silent.

"Back to work!"

Andy snickered, and Magnus sunk lower in his seat.

...

While the other children enjoyed their temporary freedom, Magnus sat on the bench with his cheese sandwich, his glass bottle of milk, a pad of paper, and the *very* sharp pencil.

It was a *very* sharp pencil. This will be important later.

Magnus scanned the play area for Abigail. He smiled as he watched her skip around with her friends. She was a pleasantly plump girl with rosy cheeks and a wide grin.

Abigail linked arms with a group of girls and they sang:

Oh my finger,
Oh my thumb.
Oh my belly,
Oh my bum.

Suddenly, out of nowhere, and without warning, Andy grabbed Magnus' blazer lapel and yanked him off the bench.

Sam called out, "Oh no. Magnus left the bench! Going to have to tell Teacher!"

"Please." Magnus begged, still clutching the pad of paper and the *very* sharp pencil.

Andy pulled Magnus close. "Please what?"

"Please just leave me alone."

"He wants to be left alone." Andy sneered. "Okay, then we'll send him to Coventry." Andy shoved Magnus to the ground, and then looked back at the toughs. "We don't speak to him, or look at him. He doesn't exist."

The toughs all nodded their agreement.

"But, first, let's give him a taste." Sam kicked Magnus in the shin. Magnus groaned, and attempted to shield himself with the pad of paper.

The boys all started chanting: "Fight! Fight! Fight!"

"Welcome to the house of whacks!" Andy shouted as he booted Magnus in the stomach.

As Magnus recoiled from the blow, time seemed to slow to a snail's pace, and he released the *very* sharp pencil that he had been holding, and it was propelled... Directly into Andy's left eye.

The pencil dropped to the ground, having served its purpose.

Andy stood stunned for approximately six seconds before he felt the throb of his wound. Andy's howl of pain was heard three miles down the road in Bulmer Tye.

Andy howled again, but this time just for show.

As though summoned by the call, the school's Headmaster Mr. Wolfe exited the school and made his way toward the furor.

The crowd quickly dispersed, leaving Andy and Magnus still sprawled on the ground.

"Boys will be boys!" Mr. Wolfe chuckled as he strolled over to the action.

Andy was crying and covering his eye with his hand, as Mr. Wolfe attempted to help him up. "Come on, let's have a look." He pulled Andy's hand away from his face, and gasped.

Andy's left eye was swollen and bloodshot, and there was a viscous, yellow liquid seeping from the outside corner.

"Straight to the nurse!" Mr. Wolfe ordered, suddenly very serious.

Mr. Wolfe turned and extended his hand to Magnus with a smile. "The glorious game of fisticuffs!"

Magnus dusted himself off, as Mr. Wolfe continued: "You may find it hard to believe, but I too was a bit of a rabble-rouser in my early days…"

Magnus shook his head in disbelief. "Not you."

"Oh yes! Young men need to get it out of their systems. Otherwise, you've got an angry man of forty brawling every chance he gets… Hitting his wife, hitting his children, staggering to the pub in the wee hours and stabbing the barkeep with a broken bottle because he didn't get the top shelf whiskey…"

Magnus' eyes were wide.

"Then comes the arrest, the trial, detention at Her Majesty's pleasure, and being subjected to things no man should ever know…" Mr. Wolfe suddenly stopped and tousled Magnus' hair. "I may have said too much."

Chapter 5

Magnus stood at the front of the classroom with a handful of notecards, obviously nervous. His sweaty palms had smudged the ink on the cards, and he squinted as he read his speech.

"This Peruvian herbaceous plant is neither a pea nor a nut..."

Magnus looked at his audience, full of blank, bored faces.

"It is a grain legume."

Teacher stood at the side, arms crossed, staring at her wristwatch.

"And, like most legumes, peanuts grow underground."

A heavy knock interrupted Magnus, and the children turned to see Mr. Wolfe standing in the doorway. He stepped into the classroom and motioned for Teacher.

Teacher followed Mr. Wolfe into the hall, and shut the classroom door behind her.

Sam pointed at Magnus. "You're in trouble."

The children all stared up at Magnus. He cleared his throat, and pushed his glasses back up his nose. "I'm not in trouble."

Teacher re-entered the classroom and marched toward the front of the room. "Magnus. Andy. Mr. Wolfe's office, post haste!"

…

Mr. Wolfe's office was smoky and dark. The blinds had been drawn, and the only sources of light were a small desk lamp, and the glow from Mr. Wolfe's pipe.

Andy sat silently, between his mum and dad, a patch covering his left eye.

Mr. Hurst, a short, squat, lump of a man, sat lifelessly in his chair, staring at his weathered hands.

Mrs. Hurst was a towering woman, with a long, thin neck that craned around to stare at Magnus as he entered the room. "The boy is a brute, and he should be locked up," Andy's mum said, as Magnus took his seat.

Mr. Wolfe leaned forward, resting his elbows on his desk. "Mrs. Hurst, in all fairness, both boys were..."

"...And his mother obviously doesn't care that her son is a deviant, or she would have attended."

Mr. Wolfe shrugged. "I wasn't able to reach her. They don't have a telephone."

Magnus sat forward in his chair. "Mum is an extremely social woman with a very full calendar."

Mrs. Hurst tilted her head at Mr. Wolfe. "I heard the mother is of unsound mind."

Mr. Wolfe cleared his throat. "Now, Mrs. Hurst… I'm not sure that's appropriate."

Mrs. Hurst learned forward. "And don't get me started on the father!"

"My father…" Magnus began quietly, "Was a pilot for the British Special Air Service." Magnus placed his right hand over his heart. "His tags were found on the white cliffs of Dover."

Mrs. Hurst shook her head and mumbled. "I heard the father's at the graybar hotel." Andy smirked.

"Now, Mrs. Hurst…" Mr. Wolfe placed his pipe in the ashtray.

"He was buried at sea," Magnus said, wistfully. "He's a hero. A dead hero, but nevertheless."

Mrs. Hurst stared at Magnus for a few seconds. It looked as though she was formulating some choice words, but she stopped herself, and took a deep breath. "I'm happy to make his mother aware of this situation."

"That won't be necessary, Mrs. Hurst." Mr. Wolfe leaned forward, and looked at Magnus out of the corner of his eye. "I will see to it."

Mr. Hurst suddenly stood up and shook Mr. Wolfe's hand, eager to make his departure. "Cheers, Wolfie."

"I think we all learned a lesson today." Mr. Wolfe coughed before continuing. "Sharp objects are extremely dangerous. I will see to it that all pencils are dulled by the end of the day."

Mrs. Hurst leaned down to Magnus. "And you…" Her eyes were squinted, and her nostrils were flared. "If you ever so much as breathe on my darling boy… That will be it!"

Mrs. Hurst grabbed Andy's hand, spun on her heel, and stormed out of Mr. Wolfe's office.

Mr. Hurst stood there for a moment, and then slowly backed out the door, leaving Magnus alone with Mr. Wolfe.

"I didn't mean to jab him in the eye with the pencil." Magnus said softly.

"I know." Mr. Wolfe put his hand on Magnus' shoulder. "Once I was drunk on whiskey, and I couldn't sleep because a magpie was cawing incessantly outside my window. Finally, I had enough, so I grabbed my rifle and went outside. I started shooting straight up into that tree, and guess what?"

"What?"

"The cawing stopped." Mr. Wolfe paused for effect. "And it turned out that I also shot down a German zeppelin on its way to bomb the Tower of London." Mr. Wolfe smiled down at Magnus. "Sometimes you just get lucky."

…

Magnus walked slowly down the path toward home, occasionally staring up at the sky. The clouds were fluffy and bright white against the blue.

It was the sort of day that contributes to high spirits, and a general feeling of optimism.

There was magic in the air, and Magnus felt it blast against his cheeks, and ruffle his hair.

As Magnus arrived home, he spotted a small package on the front step of the caravan.

There was a hand-written label on the package.

Magnus Magnusson
10 Great Cornard Road
Sudbury
Suffolk

Magnus ran his hands over the writing. He had never before received anything in the post, and this was a most exciting development.

He had a wide smile as he unlocked the door, and pushed it open. "I'm home."

Silence.

Magnus slipped off his boots and hung his coat on the rack.

As Magnus began to rip open the package, Mum wandered in, still wearing her dressing gown.

"I had a visitor this afternoon." Mum settled in her chair, obviously upset.

"Oh?" Magnus stopped, holding the paper package in his hands.

"You know I don't like visitors."

Magnus' face fell. "I do know."

"She said you intentionally stabbed her son in the eye with a pencil."

Magnus extended his pointer finger, ready to explain: "That's not entirely true…"

"You know I don't like visitors." Mum rocked gently in her chair.

"I'm very sorry."

"I don't like people coming here, and looking around, and asking questions." Mum looked over at the package in Magnus' hands. "What's that?"

"I found it outside on the step. It was addressed to me."

Mum stopped rocking. "Let me see."

Magnus walked over to Mum, and handed her the package. He watched intently as Mum inspected the parcel and then began to tear back the paper.

"What on earth?" Mum pulled out a small rectangular case.

"Please." Magnus begged.

Mum stared at Magnus. "What?"

"Would you mind terribly if I opened it?" Magnus stammered, visibly upset.

Without a word, Mum handed him the case and picked up a magazine.

Magnus sat down on the floor, took a deep breath, and slowly cracked open the case.

"Wow," Magnus pulled a beautiful silver fountain pen from the case, and twisted it between his fingers.

"It's just a pen." Mum declared bluntly.

Magnus noticed the engraving: "Agnus."

Mum looked up. "What was that?"

"Agnus." Magnus repeated.

Mum set down her magazine, suddenly concerned. "What about her?"

"The engraving on the pen says, 'Agnus.'" Magnus held up the pen. "Who is Agnus?" Magnus enquired delicately.

"Agnus was your father's mum."

Magnus' eyes widened. "My grandmother?"

"Yes."

Magnus smiled. "Does this mean that I have a grandmother who is alive and well?"

Mum stood up from her seat, shaking her head. She reached down to pick up the brown paper, and then stared at the return address. "How did she find us?"

"Mum?"

"How on earth did she find us?" Mum said, as she began ripping up the brown paper packaging. Magnus watched as the brown paper fell like snowflakes onto the carrot-colored carpet.

Chapter 6

Teacher stood at the front of the classroom, looking rather stern, holding a long ruler in both hands.

"Now children, after lunch we will be writing our letters to Father Christmas. Once you've finished writing your letter, and I feel that the penmanship is acceptable, you are to take them home and place them in your fireplace or stove." Teacher paused. "As some of you may know, when your letter burns, the magical smoke wafts up the chimney, into the sky, and up to Father Christmas. That's how he receives the message of what you'd like for Christmas."

Andy guffawed and shook his head.

"Is there a problem Andy?" Teacher slapped the ruler on her palm.

"No, ma'am."

Magnus slipped his hand up.

"Yes, Magnus?"

"What if you don't have a chimney?" Magnus asked, looking anxious.

"Well, then I suppose you could burn it in any old fire." Teacher said, but she didn't look convinced. She turned her back and began erasing the blackboard.

Sam poked Magnus in his side. "You don't have a chimney?"

Andy leaned toward Sam. "He doesn't even have a house! He lives in that decrepit, old caravan."

Magnus bit his lip, before responding: "But you should really see our summer home in the South of France. It's a grand old thing with columns and a fountain…"

Andy wagged his finger at Magnus. "More porkie pies!"

The bell buzzed.

"Run along," Teacher called, and the children quickly scattered.

Magnus opened his rucksack and pulled out the pen.

"Ahem." Teacher cleared her throat loudly. "Where did you get that pen?" Magnus turned around to find Teacher towering over him.

"It was a gift."

"It is a very nice pen. May I ask who gave it to you?"

"Agnus." Magnus sputtered nervously.

Teacher narrowed her eyes. "And who, might I ask, is Agnus?"

"She's my father's mum."

"I see…" Teacher crouched down next to his desk. "Did you steal the pen?"

Magnus shook his head. "No. It was a gift from my father's mother. I've never actually met her. In fact, I didn't know that she existed until yesterday, when I received the pen in the post. I brought it to school because I hoped to practice my penmanship during our lunch break. I want my letter to Father Christmas to be perfect."

Teacher stood up. "Well, I hope you are telling the truth, because Father Christmas hates liars."

"May I go?" Magnus asked.

Teacher looked intently at Magnus for a full five seconds, and then crossed her arms across her concave chest. "You may go."

…

Magnus stood outside the school doors, with a pad of paper tucked under his arm, and his sandwich in his hand.

Just as Magnus was about to take a bite, Andy walked past and slapped the sandwich from his hand.

"Father Christmas isn't real, you twat." Andy laughed, and then nudged Sam to laugh too. "You're a real numpty."

Magnus leaned down to pick up his sandwich, but not before Andy had a chance to give it a kick. "Aw, sorry. Didn't see it there."

Sam turned to see Mr. Wolfe exiting the school. "Wolfie is on the prowl. Let's go." The boys ran off toward the playing field.

Magnus picked up the sandwich, now covered in dirt, and dropped it into the rubbish bin.

He moved to the bench and set the pad on his lap. He pulled the fountain pen from his blazer. He stared at the pen for a moment, twisting it in his fingers, and then started to write...

I wish

A wish, of course, is a hope, or a prayer for what could be...

It is always a very good idea to have a wish ready.

Or two.

Or three!

You never know when an opportunity to make a wish will arise.

It's best to be prepared.

Magnus stared up at the sky, rubbed his chin, tapped his finger on his lip, and then finally put the pen down on the paper, and continued to write.

I wish I had a cheese sandwich.

Magnus looked up and there stood Abigail, smiling sweetly. "Where's your sammie?"

Magnus lowered his gaze. "I dropped it... It dropped."

Abigail handed him half of her sandwich. "Here. You can share mine."

"Thank you." Magnus took a small bite.

"You're welcome."

Magnus looked up at Abigail. "You have a nice face."

"Thank you." Abigail looked around the schoolyard, and then back at Magnus. "I know they've sent you to Coventry, and I know I'm not supposed to speak to you." Abigail looked around the schoolyard once more, before continuing: "But I don't really care what they say. I like you."

Magnus' cheeks flushed red. "I like you too."

Abigail looked at Magnus' pad and pen. "Are you writing your letter to Father Christmas?"

Magnus nodded.

"Well, I hope you get everything you wish for." Abigail waved as she backed away, and then ran off to find her friends.

Magnus smiled as he took another bite of the cheese sandwich. He picked up the pen, twisted it in his fingers, thought for a moment, and then started to write.

I wish I had a friend.

At that very moment, a very large boy stumbled around the corner, and ran toward Magnus waving his arms frantically.

"Oh, dear." Magnus quickly augmented the sentence, adding the word "small" between the "a" and the "friend.

35

I wish I had a ~~small~~ friend.

"Ahem." Magnus looked up, and standing directly in front of him was the smallest boy who ever was.

The boy had a friendly face, with large, wide-set eyes, round cheeks, and freckles covering the bridge of his nose.

"Hello." Magnus smiled, as he extended his hand. "I'm Magnus."

"I'm new," the boy said, staring at Magnus' open hand.

"What's your name?"

"Same as my dad's." The boy grinned mischievously.

"What's your dad's name then?" There was a just a hint of annoyance in Magnus' tone, as he dropped his hand.

"Same as mine." The boy smirked. "Only teasing. My name's Richard."

"That's a fine name. Do you know its origin? Latin? Greek?"

Richard shrugged. "I dunno."

Mr. Wolfe whistled, and waved at Richard.

"I must scurry. Mr. Wolfe's giving me the grand tour." Richard nodded in Mr. Wolfe's direction. "Nice to meet you."

"Nice to meet you too," Magnus said, gently.

Magnus looked down at the paper, and shook his head in disbelief.

He bit his bottom lip, and then started to write.

I wish I had a father.

The bell rang.

Magnus watched silently as the children made their way toward the schoolhouse. He scanned the empty playground.

As Magnus stared at the words he had written, his eyes filled with tears and his lower lip began to quiver.

"Magnus."

Magnus' mouth dropped open, and his eyes widened. He turned around slowly... And there was Mr. Wolfe, waving Magnus over. Magnus' face fell.

"What are you waiting for, chap? The bell's rung! Hurry on!" Magnus slipped the pen in his trouser pocket, and raced toward the school.

...

"Look at the little squirt!" Andy yelled, as Richard carefully edged down the school's steps. Richard pretended not to hear, as he hurried across the pavement.

Magnus tucked in behind a small shrub and watched the scene unfold. Andy and Sam were leaned against the brick wall, pointing and laughing at Richard.

"Hey half-pint!" Andy called out.

Mr. Wolfe cleared his throat, and the boys straightened up. "Boys, promise me you will leave the dwarf alone."

"Yes, Mr. Wolfe," Andy said, and Sam nodded his agreement.

As soon as Mr. Wolfe had rounded the corner, Andy and Sam pushed off the wall and ran to catch up with Richard. Andy immediately started in on him. "Hey little nipper! How'd you get so small?"

Richard looked over his shoulder, and quickened his pace when he saw Andy and Sam were trailing close behind.

Magnus carefully took off his glasses and slipped them into his rucksack, all the while keeping a close eye on the boys.

"You going to answer me?" Andy nudged Sam in the ribs, just before he launched himself at Richard. Andy grabbed Richard by the coat hood and pulled him backward, sending him tumbling to the ground.

"Stop!" Magnus screamed.

Both Andy and Sam snickered. "What are you going to do, yolky?" Sam positioned himself between Magnus and Richard.

Magnus stood a few yards from the boys, his fists clenched tight. "Mr. Wolfe told you to leave him alone."

Andy looked up at Magnus. "Yeah, well Wolfie ain't here."

"Leave him alone," Magnus said, firmly.

"Or what?" Andy stood up.

Magnus took a step forward. "Or you're going to have to contend with me."

Andy laughed, and then turned back to Richard. "This little nipper is going to answer me." Andy rolled Richard over, and leaned hard on his chest. "Now tell me little baby… How did you get so small?"

Tears formed in the corners of Richard's eyes as he looked up at Andy, and started to explain. "Well, sometimes it just happens that way. Sometimes you get someone with eleven fingers, or one leg, or hair that grows all over their backs…" Richard took a deep breath before he was able to continue, "My mum doesn't really know, but overall, I think she's quite pleased with me."

"What kind of answer is that?" Andy snarled.

"Please…" Richard begged, gasping for breath.

"Please, what?" Andy snapped, as Richard struggled under Andy's weight. Magnus watched, feeling rather helpless.

We all have these events in our lives… Where a situation presents itself, and a decision must be made.

Sometimes it involves putting ourselves in harm's way, or giving up something that we hold dear.

It can be a very difficult choice: to do something, or do nothing.

But when a situation presents itself, and there is no one watching, and you could very easily choose to do nothing and go about your day, but instead, you choose to do *something*…

That is when the magic happens.

"By the power, vested in me!" Magnus yelled as he raced toward Andy.

Andy looked over at Magnus, barreling in his direction. He quickly covered his face with both hands, allowing Richard to struggle free.

Just as he was about to reach Andy, Magnus realized he was about to become entangled in a rather messy situation. He panicked and attempted to slow his pace.

But it was rather too late.

At that exact moment, Magnus tripped on a lone shrub root and trundled forward, knocking Andy's own fist into Andy's own nose.

Upon impact, blood gurgled and spilled from Andy's nostrils. Andy touched his face, and then looked down at his bloodied hands.

"Oh, dear," Magnus looked a bit faint at the sight of blood.

Andy stood up and glared at Magnus. "You're really in for it now. I'm telling my mum!" Andy doubled back, and ran off toward home.

Magnus looked up at Sam, standing stunned and motionless a few feet away. Magnus called out. "Sam?"

Sam snapped awake, and took two steps back. He looked around the field, and then darted off in the other direction.

"Richard?" Magnus stood up and looked over at Richard, still in a heap. "Are you okay?"

Richard took a deep breath, and then nodded. "Yes." Richard turned to Magnus. "Thanks to you."

"I should get home. My mum will be…" Magnus' voice trailed off, as he brushed the debris from his trousers. "See you tomorrow." Magnus said, as he started down the path toward home.

Richard watched as Magnus walked across the field, and then disappeared around a hawthorn hedge.

As Richard slowly got to his feet, he noticed something sparkle in the grass nearby. He moved closer, and leaned down to pick the object up.

And there it was… the pen.

Richard twisted the pen around in his fingers, and read the engraving. "Agnus."

Chapter 7

Magnus hurried to the door of the caravan, shivering from the cold. He quickly kicked the debris off his boots, as he slipped his key into the keyhole.

The door was unlocked.

Magnus pushed the door open and there, in the living area, parked comfortably on the bench seat, was a squat, thick man flipping through one of his mother's political magazines.

"Where's my mum?" Magnus asked quietly.

The man looked up. They stared at each other for several seconds, before the man finally spoke. "You're a little guy, aren't you?"

Magnus stood a little straighter. "I'm of average height."

The man hulked himself off the bench, and shuffled closer to Magnus. "I'm your father." The man's voice was gruff and gravelly.

"I'm sorry." Magnus shook his head. "I thought you said you were my father."

"I *am* your father." The man smiled, but it didn't seem earnest.

Magnus stifled a laugh. "I don't think so." Magnus stood in front of the door, still wearing his coat, boots, and mittens.

The man stood in the middle of the living area, with his massive arms hanging limply at his sides, staring at Magnus. "Well, I am."

"My father was a war hero, and he was buried at sea," Magnus said calmly.

"I made you a hot drink," Mum said, as she entered the living area carrying a tray with biscuits and a teapot, interrupting the awkward exchange. "I see you've met."

"Yes." The man nodded.

Mum set the tray down on the side table, and then turned toward Magnus. "Well, don't just stand there like a coat rack. Hang up your things."

Magnus began to undress, obviously dazed, while Mum attempted a conversation with the man. "Did you have a long trip then?"

The man dipped his head once, implying that he had.

"By train, or by coach?"

"Coach." The man sat back down on the bench seat.

"I see."

Magnus watched Mum's hand shake as she poured the tea.

"Sorry." Mum set the teapot down, and perched next to the man on the bench. The man took a sip, and started sputtering. "Bloody hell! That's a hot cup of tea."

"I'm sorry." Mum picked up the plate and offered it to the man. "Biscuit?"

Magnus watched as the man took three. and immediately shoved one into his mouth.

Mum smoothed her apron, and stared down at the floor. "We're both very glad that you're here." Mum looked over at Magnus. "Aren't we Magnus?"

Magnus stood there for a moment, and then finally nodded.

...

Magnus entered the kitchen and dining area to find the table set with a linen tablecloth, fine china, and mum's silverware. The man was settled at the end of the table, with his plump arms resting on the Formica laminate top.

Magnus nodded his hello, and stood by the door, awaiting further direction.

"Sit here." The man pointed his stout, chubby finger toward the chair next to him. Magnus did as he was told.

They sat in silence for several minutes. The only noise was the odd clatter from Mum, working away in the galley area just a few feet away. Magnus stared down at his hands, folded neatly in his lap.

"You can call me Father." The man's voice croaked, and then settled into a husky baritone.

Magnus looked up at the man. His face was weathered and tired, with ruddy cheeks, deep lines, and week-old stubble. His dark and deep-set eyes were fixed outside the window, where the sun was just about to set over the East Anglian countryside.

Mum moved toward them, carrying a large casserole. She set it on the table, and picked up the lid to reveal its contents.

"Lamb."

Magnus gasped, and then quickly announced, "I'm not hungry."

"You'll eat." Mum started to dish up. "Your father was kind enough to bring this for us."

"I had a very large lunch," Magnus replied, patting his stomach.

"You'll eat." Mum set a plate down in front of Magnus. It was a lamb chop, swimming in gravy.

Mum and the man began to eat their meals.

Magnus watched Mum's face as the man cut through his lamb chop, and his knife scraped along the porcelain plate.

"Salt." The man declared, while his mouth was still full.

Mum looked up. "Sorry?"

"Needs salt." The man pointed to his plate with the sharp end of his knife.

Mum stood up quickly, and hurried to the pantry. She was back within seconds. She set the shaker down in front of the man, and then sat back down. "I'm sorry."

The man took the shaker and covered every square inch of his plate with salt.

As Mum lifted the fork to her mouth, she stopped, jumped up, and rushed back to the pantry, returning moments later with the peppershaker. "You likely wanted pepper as well."

Mum set the shaker down in front of the man, and then sat back down. "I really should have brought you both, but when you said 'salt,' I just thought salt." The man picked up the peppershaker, and doused his plate, without so much as a nod.

"What's the problem?" Mum looked over at Magnus.

Magnus stared down at his untouched plate. "I can't."

"You can." Mum hissed.

"I won't."

"You will." Mum set her fork and knife down on her plate.

Magnus' chair screeched as he stood up. "I can't, and I won't, and you can't make me." Magnus declared, as he made a hasty exit through to the living area.

"I'm so sorry." Mum apologized to the man, and then followed Magnus through to the next room.

"Magnus!" Mum waited for the flap doors to shut, and then she grabbed Magnus by the wrist and pulled him close.

Magnus looked up at Mum with those beautiful, bright, blue eyes, and Mum dropped Magnus' wrist.

"He's back." Mum kneeled down next to Magnus. "Do you understand what this means?" Her serious tone suddenly became light. "We're a family."

...

Magnus laid in his bed with the lights off, and the curtains drawn. The caravan was quiet, with the exception of the gentle tap of raindrops on the aluminum roof.

Magnus sat up in bed, and pushed the curtains aside. He looked out across the field, illuminated by the crescent moon. Sheep dotted the pasture, with their little ones snuggled close.

"We're a family."

Mum's words echoed through the room, and suddenly, Magnus' eyes widened, and he remembered...

Sitting on the bench at school, and looking down at the paper. Picking up the pen, and writing these words:

I wish I had a father.

Magnus quickly shuffled off the bed, and reached for his rucksack, hastily emptying its contents. He searched the floor, and under the cupboard, and reached as far as he could under the bed.

Nothing.

"Where is it?" Magnus muttered under his breath, as he inspected his trousers, and blazer, and then the laundry piled neatly in the corner of the room.

"Agnus sent him a package." Mum said, her words dulled from the next room.

Magnus stood very still, and then tiptoed toward the door. He turned the knob, and opened the door slowly. The door creaked, and Magnus froze as he listened.

"Oh?"

"It was a fountain pen."

Magnus' mouth dropped open.

"Oh." The man almost sounded interested.

Magnus carefully stepped out into the hallway, and then crept closer, his woolen socks padding each step.

"I don't know why she felt the need to send something." Mum's voice dropped off. Magnus peered around the corner into the living area. The flap doors to the kitchenette were open slightly, and Magnus could see Mum and the man sitting at the table. He looked over at the Big Ben clock on the sideboard. It was ten o'clock.

"I don't know what she's after," Mum said. Then she stood up and moved from view.

As soon as Mum was out of sight, Magnus sprinted to the coat rack, and scrambled to unhook his coat. He pulled it off the rack, and ran back down the hall to his room.

"Did you hear that?" Mum asked.

"Nope." The man grunted.

Magnus carefully closed the door to his room, and started hastily combing through his coat pockets. He pulled out a handkerchief, a box of matches, and a button, and then shook the coat out.

Nothing.

Magnus let the coat drop to the floor and let out an audible, exasperated sigh.

Chapter 8

The field was full of frost as Magnus sprinted toward the school, his body barely able to control the force as he negotiated the dirt path.

"Magnus!" Magnus saw Richard crest a small mound, and barrel in his direction. "Wait up!"

Magnus slowed his run, but he didn't stop.

Richard was out of breath when he finally caught up to Magnus. "You... Should see... Andy's nose!" Richard inhaled sharply before continuing. "It's swollen up like a balloon." Richard's eyes were wide and worried. "And his mum is after you."

Magnus stopped, and then pulled Richard in by the sleeve. "That's the least of my problems." Magnus looked around, and then pulled Richard close. "I lost something very important."

"Oh?"

"A pen."

Richard tilted his head. "You lost a pen?"

"Yes, a *very* special pen. A beautiful, silver pen."

"Is it valuable?" Richard asked, suddenly very interested.

"Yes. Very."

Richard bit his lip. "I haven't seen it."

"I had it yesterday, when I first met you. When I was sitting on the bench."

Richard shrugged, and avoided eye contact.

"It was given to my by my grandmother, and it's engraved with the name, 'Agnus.'"

Richard adjusted his collar, and stared down at the ground. "Why don't you just tell your gran that you lost it, and she'll get you another one?"

"Because…" Magnus looked around before he continued, "Can you keep a secret?"

"Sure." Richard croaked.

Magnus turned toward Richard. "You'll have to swear on your mum's life."

Richard nodded hastily, obviously very unaware of the implications.

"The pen is magical." Magnus whispered.

Richard laughed, but stopped abruptly when he saw that Magnus wasn't kidding. "You think the pen is magical?"

"Yes." Magnus paused. "I mean, I think so."

Richard tilted his head. "You think so?"

Magnus looked hard at Richard. "Yesterday I was writing with the pen, and all of the things that I wrote came true."

"It's called a coincidence."

"I wrote 'I wish I had a cheese sandwich,' and then Abigail gave me half of hers. Then I wrote 'I wish I had a friend,' and then you came along." Magnus got quiet and leaned in. "And then I wrote, 'I wish I had a father...'"

"Yes?"

"And then, when I got home..." Magnus paused. "He was there."

"Isn't he always there?"

"No." Magnus shook his head, and quickly wiped his eyes with his sleeve. "He's never been there."

The school bell chimed.

Richard squinted up at Magnus. "They say you lie."

"Who says?" Magnus demanded.

"All of them. Everyone. They all say you lie. About blue blood in your veins. About growing up in Greece. About your pop being a war hero. About your 'old' money..."

"Boys!" Mr. Wolfe interrupted, waving in their direction. "I hate to cut short what appears to be a wonderful exchange of thoughts and ideas, but the school bell has rung, and education waits for no one!" The boys started toward the school.

"I swear to you, Richard."

Richard didn't look convinced. "Spit your death."

Magnus spit on the ground, and made the sign of the cross on his throat. "If I lie, may I die on the spot where I spit."

"Swear on your mum."

Magnus inhaled sharply. "On my mum's life."

Richard rubbed his chin. "A magic pen?"

...

Teacher stood at the front of the class, with her pointer stick, outlining a perfect, cursive "D" on the blackboard.

"Down and around, up and over."

Magnus looked over at Andy, his lip was split, and his face was red and swollen.

"Father Christmas hates careless children," Teacher declared.

There was a knock.

Teacher set the pointer down on the ledge, and moved to the door. After a brief, muffled conversation, she stepped back into the room.

"Andy."

Magnus breathed a sigh of relief.

"And Magnus." The color drained from Magnus' cheeks as he stood up and followed Andy to the door.

...

Mr. Wolfe's office was opaque with cigar smoke as Andy and Magnus entered. Magnus looked over at Mrs. Hurst, glaring in his direction.

"Boys, have a seat," Mr. Wolfe said. Andy sat down between his mother and father.

Magnus waved the smoke out of his face, and tried to focus his eyes.

"Magnus... Have a seat next to your father."

"My father?" Magnus turned to see the man hunkered on a small, straining, wood chair, with his arms folded across his enormous chest.

"My father." Magnus declared, and suddenly it was true.

Father lifted his hand and slapped the leather seat on the chair next to him. "Have a seat, son."

Magnus climbed into the sturdy wood armchair, glancing over at Mrs. Hurst, who was still scowling.

"Spare a ciggy, Wolfe?" Father grunted.

"Of course." Mr. Wolfe handed Father a cigarette, and an antique silver lighter. Magnus watched as Father lit the roll of tobacco, and then carefully examined the lighter.

Mr. Wolfe cleared his throat before he began: "Well, you know why we're all here. It's the second altercation in as many days. I don't know what's got into the two of them... Christmas hysteria perhaps?"

"Your son is a brute," Mrs. Hurst declared heatedly. "First his eye, and now his nose! What's next? His manhood?" Mrs. Hurst exhaled loudly, and settled back in her chair.

Mr. Wolfe turned to Andy. "I had asked Andy to leave the dwarf alone. Isn't that right, Andy?"

Andy shrugged.

Mr. Wolfe cleared his throat. "Can you please shed some light on the situation, Magnus?"

"Let's see." Magnus tapped his finger on his bottom lip. "I remember that I was running, and I had my arms straight out in front of me, and then I tripped and rolled forward. I must have bumped Andy's fist into Andy's own nose." Magnus turned to Mrs. Hurst, who was fuming. "It was an unfortunate incident."

"It was absolutely premeditated," Mrs. Hurst's tone was frightfully calm. "The boy is a delinquent. A wicked little worm."

Magnus' lower lip began to quiver.

"With all due respect," Mrs. Hurst stopped, and spun around in her chair to face Father. "There's only one way to handle that kind of bad behavior."

Father took a long pull from his cigarette and then exhaled, not looking the slightest bit concerned. "Mm?"

"Flagellation!" Mrs. Hurst exclaimed proudly.

Father looked over at Mrs. Hurst, and slowly inspected her from top to toe. As Father scanned her mid-section, she straightened and blushed. Father sat forward, and stubbed his cigarette out in the ashtray. "I've heard enough out of you."

Magnus watched as Mrs. Hurst's mouth dropped open, and a little squeak escaped her lips. Magnus reveled in the moment.

"I think we all learned a lesson here today." Mr. Wolfe smiled cheerfully at Mrs. Hurst, and then at Father. "Running with your arms out in front of you is extremely dangerous, and I'm going to see it that from now on, all children run with their arms straight down at their sides!"

Mrs. Hurst glanced over at Mr. Hurst. His eyes were shut, and he was snoring quietly. She slapped the back of his head, jolting him awake. "Leonard!"

Mr. Hurst jumped up and extended his hand to Mr. Wolfe. "Ta, Wolfie."

Father leaned down to a beaming Magnus and tousled his hair. "Tell your mum I've gone to the shops."

Chapter 9

The house was quiet and dark, as Magnus let himself in the door, and stepped up into the caravan.

"Hello?" Magnus called, as he kicked off his boots, and then placed each one neatly along the wall.

"Is that you?" Mum called from the kitchen.

Magnus brightened. "Yes."

Mum entered the living room, and appeared disappointed when she saw Magnus. "Was your father at school today?"

Magnus nodded, "He asked me to tell you that he's gone to the shops."

Mum wiped her hands on her apron. "He said he'd be home by four o'clock. What time is it?"

Magnus looked over to the sideboard, where the Big Ben clock had always stood. "Where's Big Ben?"

Mum moved to the sideboard, and rested her hand on the wood shelf. "I don't know."

"Well, it couldn't have gone far." Magnus crossed the room and examined the well-worn shelf, which had become chipped, scratched and faded over its many years.

"When I was about your age my father took me to London for the day." Mum paused, allowing the memory in. "I saw the Tower of London, Buckingham Palace, and Big Ben... These sights that I had only ever read about in books." Mum turned to Magnus, her eyes wet with tears. "My father bought me that clock so I could always remember the day we spent together."

Magnus looked up at Mum, and realized that for the first time in a long time, she was dressed.

Instead of her usual dressing gown, Mum wore a long, black skirt with a navy turtleneck sweater, and slate stockings. Her hair was pulled back and pinned at the nape of her neck, and her lips were the color of ripe cherries.

"You look lovely," Magnus said gently.

Mum's gaze dropped to the floor, and she blushed. "Thank you."

...

Magnus and Mum sat across from one another at the table, eating their evening meal in silence.

Magnus pushed the baked beans around his plate, occasionally looking up at Mum expectantly.

Mum cleared her throat. "He said once he finds a job we can move into a proper house."

"Oh?"

Mum took a sip of her tea. "That's what he said."

"Will it have brick walls?" Magnus asked, hopefully.

"Maybe."

"And a fireplace?"

"Possibly."

Magnus shifted in his seat. "It would be nice to have a fireplace."

Mum nodded. "It would."

"I'm often very cold." Magnus added, under his breath.

"I know." Mum's voice dropped off.

Magnus laid his fork down on his plate. "What was she like?"

"Who?"

Magnus answered in a low voice. "Agnus."

Mum dabbed her mouth with her napkin, before answering. "She was not a kind woman. In fact, she could be downright cruel. She really didn't like me, and she didn't like your father much either."

"Oh?"

There was a creak outside, and Mum leapt up from her seat. "I'll get the door." Mum moved through to the living area, and returned moments later, looking defeated. "It must have been the wind."

...

Magnus wiped the fog from the window and stared out. The sun had just started to rise over the Cornard Tye hills.

Magnus slipped out of his pajamas and into his trousers and shirt, taking care with each and every button. He moved in front of a small mirror perched on a wood shelf, adjusted his collar, and smoothed his hair flat.

Magnus opened the door slowly and crept down the hall, trying very hard not to wake Mum.

As he entered the living area, he saw a pair of well-worn men's boots next to the front door.

And he smiled.

Chapter 10

The bell rang, and there was a quiet shuffle as the children put away their textbooks. Teacher whacked her pointer on a desk in the front row, and a hush quickly fell upon the classroom.

"Children, take note. The nativity play is tomorrow afternoon." Teacher stopped, and took a deep breath. "I want you to know your lines better than you know your name and date of birth. I do not wish to be the laughingstock of this institution. Am I making myself abundantly clear?"

"Yes, Teacher." The children answered, in relative unison.

"Class dismissed." With that, the children rushed out the door. All except Magnus, who sat at his desk with his hand raised.

Teacher turned to Magnus. "What is it?"

"I wanted to apologize for my behavior the past few days. I won't make excuses, but I can assure you that I have changed my ways."

"I should hope so," Teacher said, as she straightened a pile of papers on her desk.

Magnus cleared his throat before he continued. "I was wondering if you might reconsider your position about my participation in the nativity play?"

Teacher's eyes narrowed. "Why should I?"

"Well, it's just that I love Christmas, and I love the theatre, and it would mean a lot for me to participate in this pageant."

Teacher's stern face appeared to thaw. "Fine."

Magnus' mouth dropped open. "Fine? Really? You mean it?"

"We need a third shepherd."

. . .

As Magnus and Richard cut through the field toward home, Magnus scanned the grass and path.

Richard watched Magnus. "Still looking for your 'magic' pen?"

Magnus looked injured. "You don't believe me."

Richard was silent.

Magnus stopped and turned around to face Richard. "You still think I'm lying?"

Richard squinted up at Magnus, and nodded his head.

"Well, sometimes I do." Magnus paused. "Sometimes spinning a yarn is easier than telling the truth…" Magnus kicked a stone. "But I'm not lying about this. The pen is magical, and I have to find it."

Magnus started back down the path, with Richard trailing behind him.

"There's no point, Magnus."

Magnus shook his head. "I have to try."

"But, you'll never find it. It's like searching for a needle in a haystack."

"I have to find it!" Magnus said, as he stopped in front of the run-down, rusty caravan.

"Why?" Richard ran to catch up with Magnus. "You already got everything you wished for!"

"No, I haven't."

Richard stopped next to Magnus, and looked back at the caravan. "Do you live here?"

Magnus avoided Richard's gaze.

"Is this where you live?" Richard asked again.

Magnus' face flushed. "Yes."

…

Richard sat at the large formal dining table, with a blank pad of paper in front of him.

Richard reached across the table for the pen. He turned it over in his hand to read the engraving… *Agnus.*

Richard's mum entered with a mug in hand, and Richard quickly slipped the pen into a stack of linens. She set the mug down next to Richard and kissed the top of his head. "Are you writing your letter to Father Christmas?"

"Yes."

"Carry on then, presh." She cooed, before she made her exit.

Richard lifted the stack of linens and removed the pen. He pulled the pad close, and put the pen tip down on the paper.

Chapter 11

As Magnus sat reading a book by candlelight in the living area, he heard a clatter, a crash, and then a loud thud. Startled, he closed his book, and laid it on the table. He slowly stood up, and called out into the darkness. "Mum?"

There was no response.

Suddenly, a Christmas tree burst through the door, carried in by Father. He plopped the tree down beside the front window, and wiped his brow dramatically. "There's your tree!"

Magnus' eyes widened as he surveyed the great fir, and he clapped his hands excitedly. "We've never had a Christmas tree!"

The tree was tall, with sparse branches. Its tip had to be bent in order to accommodate the ceiling of the caravan, and its girth overwhelmed the small living room.

"Well, ya got one now."

Magnus ran his hand over the foliage. "Where did you get it?"

The question, though seemingly innocuous, appeared to unsettle Father. He looked at Magnus and snarled, "Never you mind."

His response did not seem to affect Magnus, who breathed in the tree's fresh, earthy aroma, and started dictating a list. "We'll need to get candles, and ornaments, and an angel."

"By all means." Father said, as he flopped down onto a chair. He unscrewed the top of his flask, and took a long drink.

Magnus cleared his throat. "Thank you."

Again, Magnus' words seemed to rattle Father. He took a few seconds before he finally nodded.

Magnus inched closer to Father, and then settled on the floor next to him. "They said you were buried at sea."

Father's eyes popped open. "Who said?"

"Mum." Magnus leaned in. "So you were captured?"

Father took another sip before responding. "Mm."

"By the Germans?"

Father sat up in his chair. "Yeah."

Magnus sat very still. "Were you scared?"

Father smirked. "No."

"Did you ever try to escape?"

Father looked fixedly at Magnus. "You ask too many questions."

...

Magnus stood on a chair, humming softly as he washed the dinner dishes. Mum wandered into the galley and over to the sink.

"The nativity play is tomorrow," Magnus said, quietly. "Many parents attend."

Mum looked uncomfortable. "I…" She started, but she didn't finish.

"I know." Magnus set a plate in the drying rack, and dried his hands on a towel.

Mum leaned against the counter, staring out the darkened window.

"Mum?"

"Yes?"

Magnus stepped down from the chair, and turned to Mum, his face full of worry. "Now that Father is not dead, will you still get your widow's benefits?"

"That's not for you to worry about." Mum dropped her teacup into the warm, sudsy water and promptly made her exit.

Magnus fished around in the water for the teacup, gave it a quick wash, and then placed it gently on the rack.

…

It was pandemonium in the auditorium as the children wrestled with their costumes, and their stage fright.

Magnus scanned the audience.

The boy playing Joseph stood stunned by the lights, and the girl playing Mary waved to her mum in the audience.

"And she brought forth her firstborn son and wrapped him in swaddling clothes, and laid him in a manger." Mary pulled a doll from beneath her terry cloth robe. "And there were in the same country shepherds abiding in the field, keeping watch over their flock by night."

Teacher shoved Magnus and the two other shepherds into the spotlight. Magnus cleared his throat. "Let us now go even unto Bethnal Green, and see this thing which has come to pass."

"Beth-le-hem!" Teacher barked.

"Bethlehem." Magnus repeated, flustered.

As Magnus and the shepherds shuffled toward Mary and Joseph, Magnus noticed a hulking silhouette, hidden in the shadows, leaned against the back auditorium wall.

Magnus squinted, to be absolutely, positively certain.

It was him.

...

Teacher stood at the front of the classroom, her mouth tight. "Overall, your performance was sufficient, though I wouldn't say *The Old Vic* will be calling any of you, anytime soon."

The bell rang, and the children were instantly vibrating in their seats, exceedingly eager for the holiday ahead.

Teacher kept her eyes fixed on the class.

"Now children, remember to put your letters into your fireplaces this evening, so that the magical smoke will waft up to Father Christmas."

Magnus sunk in his seat, feeling rather forlorn.

"I hope you enjoy your time with your friends and family." Teacher suddenly lowered her head, and pulled a hanky from her pocket. "As you may know, I am not presently wed. I am husbandless, and indeed companionless." Teacher wiped her eyes, and the children stared at her blankly. "I shall be spending Christmas Day in Chelmsford, with my great uncle and his wife… Who is a real nutter, but she makes a fine meal." Teacher suddenly looked up at the class, and straightened up. "Class dismissed."

With that, the children lunged toward the door. Magnus walked over to the cloakroom and began collecting his things.

"Merry Christmas, Magnus." As Magnus turned, Abigail leaned in and planted a kiss on his cheek. Magnus stood stunned for several seconds, mouth open, unable to muster a reply.

Mr. Wolfe broke the silence. "Magnus!"

"Yes, sir!"

Mr. Wolfe pushed past the other children, and crouched down next to Magnus. "I'm disappointed in you Magnus. I knew you were a bit of a storyteller, but I never took you for a thief."

"Sorry?"

"I'm sure that you are." Mr. Wolfe placed his hand firmly on Magnus' shoulder. "I would greatly appreciate its return. It was given to me by my grandfather, and it has great sentimental value."

"I'm not sure I know what you're referring to." Magnus stared down at his feet.

"My antique silver lighter. It went missing after our powwow the other day, and according to Mrs. Hurst, Andy is allergic to all metals and alums… So here we are." Mr. Wolfe lifted Magnus' chin, and waited until Magnus met his gaze. "If you can guarantee its safe return after the holidays, we won't need to discuss it any further. Understood?"

Magnus nodded.

Chapter 12

Magnus pushed open front door, stepped up into the caravan, and looked around the living area.

The area rugs had been straightened, the shoes were lined up neatly against the wall, and the sideboard had been polished to a shine. Mum's magazines had been stacked in a pile on the shelf, and her many balls of yarn were heaped in a basket.

Magnus slipped off his boots and placed them in line. He smiled when he saw the Christmas tree.

It was a sight.

The towering tree had been decorated with stringed popcorn, a few well-placed ornaments, and a handful of tinsel.

And then he spotted something far more interesting.

A present, beautifully wrapped in red paper, and adorned with a gold ribbon, sat beneath the tree.

Magnus moved closer and reached for the tag: *Magnus.*

Magnus immediately dropped the tag and ran through to the kitchen, where he found Mum, peeling potatoes at the sink.

"There's a present under the tree!"

"Lower your voice." Mum hissed.

Magnus did as he was told, whispering excitedly. "There's a present under the tree, and it has my name on the tag."

Mum was focused on the task at hand.

Magnus continued. "It's too early for Father Christmas."

"Maybe it's not from Father Christmas."

"Then who could have put it under the tree?"

Mom shrugged as she heaped the potato peelings into the rubbish bin.

Magnus began pacing the small galley. He stopped, and looked up at Mum out of the corner of his eye. "Do you think it could be from Father?"

Mum stared out the window.

"He came to my nativity play."

Mum turned around to face Magnus. "He did?"

"He did." Magnus replied, smiling.

…

Magnus rounded the corner of the caravan, and saw Father crouched down next to the support post. Magnus stood there for a moment, watching Father strain as he twisted a bolt.

"Hi."

Father dropped the wrench he was holding and bolted upright. "You spying on me?"

"No."

Father wiped his nose with the back of his hand. "What do you want?"

"I saw that there's a present under the tree." Magnus stared at Father. "And it has my name on it."

Father dipped his head.

"Is it from you?"

"Aye." Father stood up, and limped toward Magnus. "Good children…" He paused, wiping his hands on his dungarees. "That listen to their Fathers, and do as they are told, get pressies."

Magnus stared up at Father.

Father leaned down, wrapped the palm of his hand around the back of Magnus' neck, and pulled him close. "Bad children…" Father smiled through gritted teeth. "Get nought."

Magnus swallowed hard, and nodded.

Father released his grip, and patted Magnus on the cheek. "So be a good boy then." Father turned and walked back to the support post.

"I'll be good." Magnus said softly.

"You better be." Father grunted as he leaned down and picked up the wrench he had dropped.

"I saw you at school today. You came to my play."

Father leaned against the caravan, and slipped the wrench in his belt loop. "I was passing by."

"Well, I was very glad to see you there." Magnus said, and he meant it.

Magnus watched as Father started tidying up his tools, and then finally broke the silence. "Do you miss Agnus?"

Father took a moment before responding. "How do you know about her?"

"She sent me a gift. There may have been a letter, but I never got to read it."

Father suddenly became agitated. "You don't say."

Magnus looked up at Father. "You must miss her."

Father didn't answer. His gaze was fixed on the wrench in his hand.

"And I bet she misses you too."

…

Magnus strained as he reached inside a small cupboard, and pulled out several pieces of crumpled brown paper.

He began placing the fragments of paper together, lining up the return address so that it could be read.

He smoothed the paper down, and his fingers traced the address.

Agnus Magnusson
Number 6 Mill Road
Marks Tey
Suffolk,

Chapter 13

The rain poured down as Magnus hurried toward the grand wood doors of a palatial home. He strained as he reached for the cast-iron doorknocker in the shape of a lion's head. Magnus grabbed the ring, and struck the plate twice. He took two steps back and stared up at the lion's head.

The door finally opened, and a lanky and looming man peered down at him. "Yes?"

"Hi, I'm Magnus." Magnus extended his hand, but the man did not take it. "I'm looking for Richard."

"Master McNaulty is indisposed," the tall man said, as he extended his arm across the door's frame.

"Magnus?" Richard peeked around the corner, obviously anxious. "What are you doing here?"

"I have to talk to you."

Richard pushed past the wall of a man, and hurried toward Magnus. "What is it?"

"Master McNaulty, return to the parlor at once."

Richard pulled Magnus close and whispered, "Go down to the big barn. I'll be there as soon as I can."

"Forthwith, Master McNaulty, forthwith!" With that, the tall man reached down, plucked Richard up in his arms, and carried him back into the house.

"Good day!" The man yelled over his shoulder at Magnus.

. . .

The door creaked as Magnus pushed inside the darkened barn, scarcely lit by the cracks in the eaves.

"Hello?" Magnus called, fearing that someone, or something, was lurking.

Magnus started to close the barn door, and then opted to leave it ajar. He settled himself on a bale of hay, and looked around the immense space. There was old farm equipment, bundles of firewood, and empty stalls where animals had once found shelter.

"I know why you're here." Richard's voice was raspy, like he had just been crying.

"You know why I'm here?" Magnus turned and saw Richard slip through the barn doors.

"Yes." Richard sat down next to Magnus, and folded his hands on his lap.

"You know that I need your help to find my grandmother?" Magnus asked, in disbelief.

"That's why you're here?" The relief was instant, and Richard exhaled audibly.

"I want to find my grandmother and bring her home to be with my family for Christmas."

"That's why you're here!"

Magnus nodded.

Richard looked at Magnus. "How will you find her?"

"She wrote to me, and the return address was in Marks Tey. It's just a few stops on the train. Will you come with me?"

"When?"

"Now." Magnus stood up.

Richard stared down at his hands, avoiding Magnus' gaze. "I have a piano lesson at ten."

"We can leave as soon as you're finished."

A pitiful, petulant sigh escaped from Richard's mouth. "But, what will I tell my mum?"

"Tell her anything," Magnus shot back.

"Well, I can't tell her I'm with you."

Magnus looked injured. "Why not?"

Richard finally looked up at Magnus. "Andy's mum came around."

"Oh?"

Richard nodded. "She told my mum that you're a bad seed, and said if we're mates, we'll both end up in prison… Just like your father."

"My father wasn't in prison. He was a prisoner of war."

Richard shrugged. "I dunno."

"You do know. Because I've told you." Magnus moved toward the door, and then turned back to Richard.

"That's what Mrs. Hurst said."

"She's obviously got her wires crossed." Magnus sniffed, and then wiped his eye with his sleeve. "And I'm not a bad seed. You know that I'm not."

Richard nodded.

"I'm your friend, and I could use your help."

Richard stood up. "I'll meet you at the churchyard in an hour."

…

Magnus moved quickly through the churchyard, past the mausoleums and tombs covered with withered and exhausted flowers. As he walked past a giant Gospel Oak, he spotted a lone magpie perched on one of its branches.

"One for sorrow, two for joy." Magnus mumbled under his breath. A second magpie swooped in to join the first, and Magnus sighed with relief.

As Magnus settled on a bench, he noticed a funeral procession move through the graveyard. There were several women, dressed in black, all huddled together. Their bodies shuddered as they wept.

"Are they laughing or crying?" Richard whispered, startling Magnus, who hadn't heard him approach.

Magnus looked over his shoulder at Richard, leaning on the back of the bench. "They're crying."

"Why?"

"You see that wood box?" Magnus pointed to the casket at the edge of the churchyard.

Richard nodded.

"Someone they love is in there." Magnus said gently. "And they have to say goodbye." The boys watched as the procession gathered around the casket.

Richard shifted his weight on the bench. "Mum says if you're a believer, you go up to heaven to have a party with Jesus Christ, God, and the Holy Ghost. If you're not a believer, you go straight to hell in a hand basket." Richard paused. "Guess if they are crying, he's going to hell."

"One or the other." Magnus responded, as he hopped down from the bench.

As the boys walked through the churchyard, Magnus surveyed the cars in the cavalcade.

"Are you counting the cars?" Richard asked.

Magnus dipped his head with a nod. "Eleven."

"Counting cars is bad luck." Richard said solemnly.

"It is?"

"Yes. Now you have to hold your collar until you see a black dog and a white horse."

Magnus turned around to face Richard. "Who told you that nonsense?"

"My cousin knew a girl that counted cars at a funeral…" Richard leaned in close. "The next day she was dead."

"The next day?"

"The very next."

Magnus reached up and took hold of his collar.

…

As soon as the train pulled into the Sudbury station, Magnus and Richard pushed off the brick wall and eagerly climbed aboard the carriage. They rushed down the aisle and quickly found their seats.

"Have your tickets at hand please."

Magnus looked up and saw the Ticketing Officer making his way in their direction, checking tickets. "Oh, dear."

Richard fidgeted with his coat buttons. "What are we going to do, Magnus?"

"Allow me."

The boys avoided eye contact as the slight and irritable man stopped next to them. "Tickets please."

Magnus looked up at the man, and smiled. "You might be wondering where our tickets are."

"I might indeed," the man snapped.

"My mum has our tickets in her handbag, and I'm afraid she's all the way at the other end of the train."

The man rolled his eyes. "You must think I'm a right cabbage."

"Oh no, not at all." Magnus shook his head.

"Everyone needs a ticket." The Ticketing Officer started writing in his book.

"You see, we're en route to Marks Tey to see her physician, because she's suffering from... How shall I say this delicately?" Magnus tapped his finger on his lip, and then held it up in the air. "Oh, that's right... Camp fever. Typhus. Gastroenteritis. She told us to stay far, far away from her, so we're here, all the way at the other end of the train."

The Ticketing Officer pursed his lips. "Right. I see."

Magnus nudged Richard. "I thought you might."

"I trust you boys will be on your best behavior."

"We are nearly always on our best behavior."

...

"Are we there yet?" Richard sighed.

"Do you see a house?" Magnus asked, still holding his shirt collar.

"No."

"An igloo?"

"No."

"A tee pee?"

"No."

"Well then, I believe you have answered your own question." Magnus said sharply.

"It's cold." Richard whined.

Magnus walked a few paces ahead of Richard, urging him forward. "It can't be much further."

"What was the house number?"

"Six."

Magnus looked to the side of the road, where there was a small sign post sticking up out of the overgrown hedge: *6*.

"This must be it." Magnus said, as his eyes followed the well-beaten path... To an empty lot, littered with rubbish. The property appeared to have been recently vacated, and the clearing had fresh tire tread marks leading to the road.

"Where's the house?" Richard stood next to Magnus, his hands on his hips.

"I don't know." Magnus descended the small slope to get a better look at the plot.

"Where's your grandmother?"

"I don't know." Magnus slumped on a tree stump, defeated. "I wanted to get him a present. I wanted to make him happy." Magnus bit his lip, holding back tears. "I wanted it to be the happiest Christmas that ever was."

Richard moved closer and passed Magnus a handkerchief. "Let's go home."

…

Magnus unlocked the door, and let himself into the caravan. The living area was dark and silent.

"Magnus, is that you?" Mum said, in a hushed, low tone.

Magnus tried to focus his eyes in the dim room. "Yes."

"Your father went out looking for you."

"He did?"

The light snapped on, illuminating the room.

Magnus turned to see Mum rocking in her chair. Next to her sat an older woman, slight in stature, with a shock of short blue-gray hair, and a big smile.

And when I saw him my heart leapt out of my chest, and into my throat.
I couldn't speak.
He was such a beautiful baby, and now he was such a beautiful boy.

Chapter 14

"I remember the day he was born…"

"Who?" Magnus slipped off his boots, and moved closer, completely captivated by the woman.

"He had a full head of flaxen hair, and those bright, blue eyes." She smiled as she remembered.

Magnus kneeled down at her feet. "Who?"

"He was the most beautiful baby."

"Who?"

The woman looked down at Magnus and beamed. "You."

Magnus leaned in. "Are you Agnus?"

The woman nodded.

"You're my grandmother."

"Yes, I am."

Magnus looked over at Mum, who was looking rather stern. "This is going to make him so happy."

Mum shook her head. "He's not happy... Not happy at all."

Agnus reached down and took Magnus' hand. "I have something very important to tell you."

"Yes?" Magnus studied Agnus' open, friendly face. He looked at the lines around her eyes, and imagined that they were all from smiling. "What is it that you have to tell me?"

Agnus looked down at the floor, and then back up at Magnus. "Oh, dear. I can't remember at the moment." She paused. "But it will come back to me."

Mum grabbed Magnus by the hand. "Magnus, come." She pulled him into the dining area, and closed the door.

"It's a Christmas miracle!" Magnus declared, as Mum crouched down next to him.

"It's a disaster. Your father is furious that she showed up here, unannounced, and uninvited."

Magnus' eyebrows furrowed. "He's not happy to see her?"

"No."

"But she's his mum."

Mum stared down at the floor. "He said she's off her trolley, and she needs to be put away."

"But she's his mum." Magnus got quiet. "And she's my grandmother."

"She'll be gone in the morning." Mum stood up quickly. "In the meantime, he wants you to stay away from her."

"She said she had something important to tell me."

"She's got nothing to tell you. She's as batty as a belfry." Mum pushed open the door, and then turned back to face Magnus. "Where were you this afternoon?"

Magnus crossed his fingers behind his back, and looked up at Mum. "I was playing football with some mates and lost track of the time."

Mum nodded, but looked suspicious. "Go to bed."

Magnus moved toward the hall, and peeked into the living area. Agnus sat on the bench seat, staring straight ahead at the Christmas tree.

…

Magnus stared out the front window, and watched as Father and Agnus made their way along the icy path to the road. "Where is he taking her?"

"Home."

Magnus watched as Agnus gripped Father's arm. "But she doesn't have a home."

"Stop your nonsense. The woman has a home."

Magnus turned back and looked at Mum, who was rocking in her chair, reading a political magazine. "I would have thought he would have been happy to see his mum."

Mum sighed, and laid aside her magazine. "I guess he doesn't like surprises."

Magnus wiped the frost from the window with the side of his hand, and stared out.

"Magnus."

Magnus smiled at Mum. "Yes?"

"There's washing to do."

…

Magnus closed the door of the caravan, locked the door, and then checked to make sure it was latched. He picked up the large washing bag and tossed it over his shoulder, shuddering under its weight.

"Hi." Magnus turned to see Richard standing at the foot of the steps. "I was going to knock, but I remembered that your mum doesn't like visitors."

"So you've just been waiting?"

"Yes."

"In the cold?"

"Yes." Richard pulled his wool cap down over his ears, and followed Magnus down the icy path. "I got in a whole load of trouble for yesterday. My mum almost called the bobbies. She thought I was dead."

Magnus negotiated the path carefully. "I'm sorry."

"She doesn't want us to be friends anymore."

"That's unfortunate." Magnus said, and he meant it.

"If she caught me with you, I'd get the cane and slipper." Richard struggled to keep up to Magnus. "So I told her I'm with Andy."

Magnus smiled, and slowed his pace so that Richard could keep in step. "When I got home last night, Agnus was there, sitting in the living room with Mum."

"Blimey." Richard grinned. "So you'll have your happy Christmas yet."

"Unfortunately, my father was not as happy to see her." Magnus said, reflecting on the previous evening.

"But she's his mum!"

"He says she's barking mad, and needs to be locked up… But I thought she was rather lovely and kind."

…

Richard sat next to the washing machine, his feet dangling off the chair, listening intently to Magnus.

"He was a pilot in the British Special Air Service." Richard's eyes were wide, as Magnus continued to spin his yarn. "The Germans shot his plane down, but he still managed to land it safely on a beach near Berlin, using only his keen sense of direction. He tried to swim to Sweden, but those bastards had a submarine and found him treading water in the Baltic Sea. They captured him and threw him in the chokey."

"He told you this?"

"Pretty much."

Richard tilted his head. "Pretty much?"

"Bits and pieces." Magnus unloaded the machine, pushing the wet clothes back into the washing bag. "He's a man of very few words."

Magnus threw the washing bag up over his shoulder, and the boys exited the launderette.

The rain had stopped, the fog had lifted, and the sky had turned a shade of pink reminiscent of flushed, or pinched cheeks.

The boys strolled along the High Street, admiring the Christmas decorations adorning the shop fronts and the elaborate window displays.

As Magnus and Richard walked past the Jeweler's window display, something stood out amongst the treasures and trinkets.

Magnus handed Richard the washing bag, which nearly toppled him, and moved closer to the window. "That looks just like my mum's clock."

The door chimed as Magnus stepped inside. A small, weaselly man with wide, bulging eyes came out from a back room.

"I'm enquiring about the Big Ben clock in the window."

"Lovely, isn't it?" The words slid out of the man's small, pursed mouth.

"It is." Magnus clasped his hands together. "May I ask how you acquired it?"

The man leaned against the counter. "I was asked to be discreet."

"I see." Magnus scanned the cases of rings and watches. "My mum had one just like it. I'd love to replace it for her. What are you asking?"

"Twenty pounds."

"Right." Magnus coughed, taken aback. "Thank you sir." Magnus bowed, and backed out of the store.

…

The sun was just setting over Great Henny hill as the boys walked through the field toward home.

Richard looked up at Magnus. "I have to tell you something."

"What is it?" Magnus didn't seem bothered.

"You have to promise not to get angry."

"Okay."

"Promise?"

"Yes."

Richard blew warm air on his cold hands. "You say, 'yes,' but I think you might get very angry."

"I'm not really the sort of person who gets very angry." Magnus said, as he sidestepped an icy puddle.

"After I tell you, you might be the sort of person that gets very angry."

Magnus stopped, and turned to Richard. "What is it?"

Richard's cheeks flushed red, and he shook his head. "It's nothing."

"It sounded like something."

"It wasn't." Richard tugged his wool cap lower.

Magnus started down the path again. He stepped on a frozen puddle, breaking the ice. "You sure?"

Richard nodded, as the boys arrived to Pot Kiln Road. "I should get home." He took a step back, and then stopped. "Merry Christmas, Magnus. I'm glad that you got everything you wanted."

Magnus' eyes followed Richard as he ran off toward home.

Chapter 15

Magnus sat on a fence post next to the caravan, looking out to the pasture, where several sheep were grazing in the frosted grass. A few sheep took shelter under a leaning crack willow tree.

Magnus noticed that one sheep standing under the tree was very still, and seemed to be staring straight back at him.

"Hello, old friend." Magnus called out to the sheep.

A blast of cold air caused Magnus to shiver, and he sunk deeper in his coat.

"Magnus."

Magnus turned around to see Agnus walking up the driveway toward him, and a blue police car slowly pulling away.

She waved in his direction. "Hello, my darling dear."

Magnus hopped down, and brushed the debris from the back of his trousers. "You're back."

"Yes." Agnus pulled a ring of keys from her coat pocket. She chose one, and tried to put it into the lock on the caravan's front door. It didn't fit. "I had to come back because I have something very important to tell you."

"What is it?"

Agnus tried another key in the lock. "I just have to remember."

"Was it about the pen?"

Agnus turned to Magnus. "You received the pen?"

"I did." Magnus said, nodding.

Agnus leaned toward Magnus. "It's a very special pen, you know."

"I do know."

"It is very special because…" Agnus' voice trailed off, as she stared at the keys in her hands.

"…It's magic."

Agnus looked confused. "What is?"

"The pen." Magnus whispered. "Everything I wished for, and wrote down with it, came true."

Agnus tried another key in the lock.

"I wished for a sandwich, and for a friend." Magnus became quiet. "And then I wished for a father… And then he came back."

Agnus reached for Magnus' hand. "Your father came back because he had nowhere else to go."

Magnus reached for Agnus' hand. "I think you're confused. He fought in the war, and we thought he was buried at sea, but he was captured by the Nazis."

"Nazis?" Agnus laughed, and then quickly stopped when she saw the earnest look on Magnus' face. "My sweet dear." Agnus put her hand on Magnus' shoulder. "Your father is no hero, and he did not fight in any war. He was locked up in Liverpool on a smash and grab."

Magnus pushed Agnus' hand away. "No, you've got it wrong. You're confused. Mum says you're confused. He was captured and locked up by the Nazis. He's a hero. You just don't remember."

It's true.
But, every now and then, a memory will be so clear and so bright...
It's like looking at a photograph, with every detail in Kodachrome.

Agnus took another key from the ring, and tried it in the lock. It didn't fit.

"What are you doing?" Magnus took a key from his pocket and put it in the lock. He turned the key and the door opened.

"My home looked just like this one." Agnus stared at the exterior of the caravan. "But it's not this one, is it?"

Magnus shook his head solemnly. "No."

"One day I came home and it was gone." Magnus helped Agnus up the steps and inside. "I think he took it."

…

Magnus stood at the open front door, watching as Father helped Agnus up into the passenger side of a Bedford K dropside truck. The engine was running, and black plumes of smoke trailed out of the exhaust pipe.

"Will she be alright?" Magnus tried to get a look at the driver, but the windows of the truck were fogged.

"Shut the door. It's freezing." Mum said, as she pulled a woolen blanket up over her legs.

Magnus shut the door and moved to the front window. He watched as Father climbed into the truck next to Agnus, and slammed the door shut. "Will she be alright?"

"She'll be fine. He's taking her home."

The truck pulled away, and Magnus turned around to Mum. "She told me she doesn't have a home."

"Nonsense." Mum snapped.

"She said she used to have a caravan, just like ours."

"Hm."

"She thinks he took it."

"She's just a confused, old woman."

"I know she is." Magnus settled on the floor next to Mum's feet. "She also said Father was locked up in Liverpool on a smash and grab. But I told her it wasn't true."

Mum's chair stopped rocking.

"I told her she was just confused… I told her that he was captured by the Nazis, and he's a hero." Magnus looked up at Mum. "I told her."

Mum's face drained of all color, as she pulled a magazine from the pile and began leafing through the pages.

Chapter 16

Magnus quickly crawled into bed, settled his head, and pulled the blanket up around his face. He took a deep breath. The vapor was visible in the cold of the room.

A light from outside refracted along the stippled ceiling. Magnus sat up, and peeked up over the window's sill. Magnus saw a set of headlights, and watched as they paraded down the road and stopped out front.

Magnus' eyes widened as Agnus climbed out of the car and waved at the driver.

Magnus jumped out of bed, and ran to his door. He pushed it open carefully, and soundlessly.

There was a knock at the door, and Magnus heard Father's thunderous footsteps move across the living area, shaking the whole caravan. He heard the door unlatch and the creak of its hinges, and then:

"Bloody hell!"

…

As Magnus stood on a chair at the sink washing the breakfast dishes, Agnus entered the kitchen.

"Sweet Magnus."

Magnus turned and greeted Agnus with a wide smile. He wiped his hands on a towel, and stepped down from the chair. "Mum told me you had left."

"I'm not supposed to talk to you. I'm supposed to wait outside. But I wanted to say goodbye." Agnus wiped her eyes with the back of her hand. "I have to go away again."

Magnus forced a smile. "He's going to take you home."

Agnus moved closer to Magnus, and touched his cheek. "Sweet Hope. You deserve so much more, and yet you are content." Agnus said, as she held Magnus' face in her hands.

Tears began streaming down her cheeks. "Please, never lose that bright-eyed hope."

I remember the day he was born. He had a full head of flaxen hair, and those bright, blue eyes.

He was such a beautiful baby, and now he is such a beautiful boy.

"Agnus!" Father's voice boomed through the paper-thin walls of the caravan. "Where are you?"

"I have to go." Agnus kissed the top of Magnus' head. "But I'll come back soon to see you."

Magnus lowered his head. "When?"

Agnus squeezed Magnus' hand. "When the time is right."

Father stormed into the kitchen, and grabbed Agnus roughly by the arm. "Let's go, woman." Father pulled Agnus out of the kitchenette, through the living room, and out the front door, slamming it shut behind them.

Magnus ran to the window and watched as Agnus struggled down the icy steps.

"Hurry it up!" Father shouted.

The same Bedford K dropside truck was idling on the road. The driver wasn't visible from the window, so Magnus ran to the door and opened it a crack.

As Father pushed Agnus up into the truck's cab, he spoke to the driver. "You know you're the only one for me, love. I'm only playing happy family until I can get them out of the caravan." Magnus' eyes widened, as Father continued. "The wench just doesn't leave. Sends the kid out for everything. Even the washing." Father paused, listening. "As soon as I can get them both out of the caravan, I'll call for you." Father leaned into the truck. "But first, take this one as far as you can away from here. Into the woods, or out to sea. I don't care… As long as I never see her again."

Father looked back at the caravan, and tilted his head, like he had seen something.

Magnus immediately shut the front door, and ran down the hallway to his room, closing the door behind him. He moved to the side of his bed, and kneeled down beside it. He folded his hands, closed his eyes, and took a deep, sharp breath.

"Please."

Magnus listened carefully, and heard nothing. He exhaled, allowing his body to relax.

There was a knock at the door.

Magnus straightened up. "Hello?"

"Can I come in?" Father's voice was hushed, and low. Before Magnus could answer, the door swung open, and Father stepped inside the small room. He looked around before finally speaking. "What did you hear?"

Magnus swallowed hard. "Nothing."

"It seemed like you heard something."

"I didn't."

Father grabbed Magnus by the ear and pulled him very close. "I hope you're not lying to me."

Magnus shook his head. "No."

"Because if there's one thing I hate, it's a liar." Father let go of Magnus' ear, which was now red and sore. Father started toward the door and then stopped. "Do you want to have a happy Christmas?"

Magnus nodded, and tried very hard not to cry.

"Then keep your mouth shut."

...

Magnus walked down the street, carrying a small sack of groceries. The village was lit up with Christmas cheer, but Magnus didn't appear to notice.

As he moved past the Jewelry Store, he stopped to look at the Big Ben clock, still featured prominently in the window display.

Suddenly, Magnus' mouth dropped open. There, in the window, next to Big Ben, was Mr. Wolfe's antique silver lighter.

The bell chimed as Magnus stepped inside the shop.

The weasel-faced Jeweler looked up from his loupe, and stared at Magnus. "Hello, young man. Weren't you in here the other day, admiring that clock?"

"I was."

"For your mum?"

Magnus dipped his head. "Yes. She had one just like it."

"And you'd like to replace it for her?"

"I would."

The Jeweler went over to the window display, and retrieved the clock. He set it on the counter, and held out the price tag. "Twenty pounds."

"I was also admiring the antique lighter in the display." Magnus gestured in the direction of the window.

The man looked smug as he moved toward the display, and returned with the lighter. "It's genuine silver."

The man handed the lighter to Magnus, who inspected it closely. "I know someone that would appreciate this."

"The lighter is just five pounds."

Magnus was undeterred. "Thank you."

"Shall I wrap them for you?" As he asked the question, his eyes seemed to bulge out further.

"Please." Magnus strolled around the shop, as the man quickly wrapped the two parcels.

"Would you like a Christmas bow on each?"

"Please."

The man finished wrapping the gifts and set them on the counter. "Just the issue of payment then."

"Ah, yes. The issue of payment." Magnus strode over to the counter, and tried hard to maintain his composure. "Forgive me, but I'm sure that you're aware that marketeering, or, the handling of stolen goods, is a crime punishable by law."

"Sorry?" The man scoffed.

"I'm sure that you are." Magnus looked up at the man, and stood up straight. "It's unfortunate that you were involved in such unprincipled dealings. So, tell you what... I will happily return this clock to my mum, and the lighter to its rightful owner."

The man pursed his lips, and scowled at Magnus.

"And you…" Magnus stared firmly at the man. "Can avoid detainment at Her Majesty's Pleasure."

The man shoved the packages toward Magnus, and spun on his heel. "Adieu."

Chapter 17

Magnus kneeled down next to his bed, holding the two wrapped packages from the jeweler. He lifted his blanket and pushed the larger one as far as he could under the bed's frame.

"Where did you take her?" Mum asked, her words only slightly muffled by the thin wall.

"You ask too many questions."

Magnus quickly pushed the smaller wrapped package under the bed. He moved to his door and slowly opened it, as the conversation between Mum and Father continued.

"Belt up, woman." Father growled, as Magnus crept down the hallway toward the living room, and peeked around the corner.

Mum was pacing the small living area. "What have you done with her?"

"You keep your nose where it belongs," Father hollered.

Mum was crying now. "Why did you not want us to talk to Agnus?"

"Did you not hear me, woman?" Suddenly, Father turned and looked straight at Magnus. His eyes were wide and full of fury. "You little sneak. You've been listening again?"

Magnus stood up straight, too scared to speak.

Father stretched his neck out, and then leaned down to Magnus. "What did you hear?"

"I don't know."

"I think you might be a teller of untruths…" Father grunted, as he crouched down next to Magnus. His teeth were yellowed and chipped, and his breath smelled like egg sandwiches. "I asked you before, and I'll ask you only once more… What did you hear?"

Magnus had once heard that if you have an encounter with a wild animal, you should make yourself very small, and stay very still.

Magnus stood very still.

He stared off into the distance, past Father, out the window, into the field, where a baby lamb followed its mother to the water trough for a drink.

"You better answer me boy." Father's tone was eerily calm.

"Mum asked you where you took Agnus."

Father tilted his head. "So you did hear?"

Magnus lowered his head.

"So you're a liar."

Magnus bit his quivering lower lip.

"Son." Father lowered his voice. "I don't like liars, and I don't like sneaks."

Mum wiped her tears with her apron. "Please leave him alone."

Father got to his feet, and turned to Mum. "He probably nicked that clock of yours."

Magnus tried to meet Mum's gaze. "No, I didn't!"

"Come here." Father hissed, grabbing Magnus by the arm, and pulling him close. "Don't you want to have a happy Christmas?"

Magnus stared at the Christmas tree. The Christmas tree candles had been lit, casting a soft glow on the room.

"Don't you want to have the happiest Christmas that ever was?" Father asked, as he let go of Magnus' arm.

Magnus looked into Father's deep, dark eyes and then back at Mum.

Mum nodded at Magnus solemnly, and then moved through to the kitchen galley, the doors flapping gently behind her.

"Then we'll need the biggest goose that ever was." Father rubbed his hands together. "So go get it."

Magnus moved to the door, and slid his foot into his boot. "I don't have any money."

Father smirked. "Nick it."

Chapter 18

Huddled deep in his warmest coat, Magnus hurried down the sidewalk, navigating his way through the throngs of shoppers on the busy High Street.

"Merry Christmas!" A very tall and well-dressed man tipped his hat to Magnus.

"Merry Christmas, Mr. Hughes." Magnus replied, forcing a smile.

A young woman pushing a pram waved at Magnus. "Merry Christmas." Magnus waved, and carried on.

As Magnus rushed through the crowd, he sidestepped a small child in order to avoid a collision, and slipped on a patch of ice. He tumbled backward, and collapsed in a heap.

He lay there for a moment, flat on his back, staring up at the stars sparkling in the sky.

And he tried very hard not to cry.

"Whene'er I wander, at the fall of night,
Where woven boughs shut out the moon's bright ray,
Should sad Despondency my musings fright,
And frown, to drive fair Cheerfulness away,
Peep with the moon-beams through the leafy roof,
And keep that fiend Despondence far aloof."

"Magnus." Abigail's dulcet tone was music to his ears. "You poor thing." Abigail extended her hand, and helped Magnus to his feet. "What happened?"

Magnus tried to find the words to say what had, indeed, happened.

But it was all too much.

And his eyes… They said it all.

Abigail pulled Magnus close, and wrapped her arms around his waist in a tight embrace. "Oh, sweet Magnus… You'll be alright." Magnus rested his head on her shoulder. "I promise."

…

Magnus peered through the window of the butcher's, which was packed to the gills as the masses acquired their holiday roasts.

As he stared up at the goose carcasses hanging in the window, the door chimed and out stepped Richard and his mother.

Richard spotted Magnus, and immediately pulled his mother in the opposite direction.

"Richard!" Magnus called.

Richard pretended he didn't hear him, and continued to urge his mother forward.

"Darling, please." Richard's mother released Richard's hand, and moved in the other direction. "I'm going to nip into the chemists. Back in a jiff."

"Richard!" Magnus shouted, chasing after Richard.

"You know." Richard turned around to Magnus. "You know, don't you?"

Magnus stood still, and waited for Richard to continue.

"About the pen." Richard's gaze was fixed on the ground.

"What about it?" Magnus asked quickly.

"It isn't magic."

"How do you know?"

Richard finally looked up at Magnus. "I know."

Magnus asked again, speaking very slowly. "How do you know, Richard?"

"I found it in the field, that day, when Sam and Andy came after me." Richard kicked a rock on the pavement. "When I found it, I didn't know it was yours."

"But, you knew I was searching for it."

Richard bowed his head. "I wanted to try it. I wanted to see if it was really magical."

Magnus took a deep breath. "Where is it?"

Richard took a step back from Magnus. "It's not a magical pen. I tried it. It didn't even write. The nib was busted."

"Richard, where is it?" Magnus demanded.

"I binned it."

Magnus winced at Richard's words. "You did what?" Magnus steadied himself against a brick wall.

"Please don't be angry with me." Richard pleaded.

Magnus shook his head, crestfallen.

Richard attempted a reprieve. "You don't need it anyway. You already got everything you wished for."

Richard's Mum strolled over to the two boys, and pulled Richard into an embrace. "Is this a new friend?"

"Yes. This is Magnus."

Her smile quickly faded. "We really must go, my darling. I must get on with Christmas preparations." She smiled at Magnus. "Nice to meet you, my dear." She took Richard's hand and they started walking away.

Richard turned back to Magnus. "You don't need it anyway. You already got everything you wanted."

Magnus watched as Richard's mum pulled him close, pushed the damp hair aside, and kissed him on the forehead.

Magnus shook his head. "No, I didn't."

Chapter 19

The old moon was shining bright in the night sky, as Magnus stood outside the front door of the caravan, and took a deep breath.

He took the key from his pocket and unlocked the front door. The living area was dim and quiet, and Mum was relaxed on the bench seat, focused on her knitting. Magnus let out a sigh of relief.

"No Christmas goose?" Mum asked calmly.

Magnus shook his head. "Butcher was out."

"Oh." Mum's voice was almost a whisper. "I don't much like goose anyway."

"Me neither." Magnus slipped off his boots and coat, and crossed the room. He sat on the floor next to Mum, and listened to the needles as they clicked gently with each stitch.

"Mum."

"Yes, Magnus?"

"Why are you sad?"

Mum laid her knitting needles in her lap. "I don't know." Mum looked over at Magnus. "I wish I wasn't."

Magnus shuffled closer to Mum and rested his head on her knee. Mum reached her hand out to touch Magnus' head, and then, suddenly...

The entire caravan shifted abruptly to one side, and both Mum and Magnus tumbled to the floor.

A single ball of gray yarn rolled off the side table, onto the floor, and came to rest in the middle of the room.

"What was that?" Mum asked, but she knew.

...

Magnus set the table carefully, making sure that the salad and dinner forks were correctly positioned to the left of the plate, and the dinner knife on the right pointed inward.

Mum and Father were having a heated discussion in the next room, and Magnus tried his best to ignore it.

Magnus held up a spoon for inspection, and noticed a watermark. He breathed on it, and rubbed it with a cloth napkin.

"Why did you come back here?" Mum asked, her words echoing through the caravan. "What do you want from us?"

Magnus set the spoon down and moved closer to the wall. He pressed his ear against the wood panel and listened.

"What were you doing under the caravan?" Mum persisted.

"What did I just say?" Father growled.

Magnus peeked through the flap door into the living area. Mum stood in the center of the room, with her arms hanging limply at her sides.

"Belt up, woman." Father stood with his hands on his hips, his face just inches from Mum's. He was sloshed on whiskey, and swaying slightly.

Magnus looked past Mum and Father, to the sideboard, and noticed that Mum's Big Ben clock was back in its rightful place. Magnus' eyes narrowed.

"Maybe Agnus isn't off her rocker. Maybe what she said to Magnus was true."

"What did I tell you, woman?" Father roared.

Magnus watched intently as Father slowly raised his hand, high up in the air.

And then everything went silent.

There are moments when it seems as though darkness has won... When "life presents no bloom."
Do not believe it.
Not even for a second.
Because the light *always* wins.
"Chase him away, sweet Hope, with visage bright,
And fright him as the morning frightens night!"

Mum stood in the middle of the room, looking very calm.

There were no tears, and no sorrow...

Just an awakening.

"Get out." Mum's voice cracked.

Father laughed. "Or what?"

"Get out." Mum repeated herself, and she stood straighter.

Father stumbled toward Mum, and grabbed her by the arm. "What are you going to do?"

At that moment, Magnus burst into the living room, grabbing the Big Ben clock from the sideboard and wielding it like a weapon. "Unhand her!"

Father let go of Mum's arm, and glared at Magnus. "You little sneak! Listening in again." Father spotted the Big Ben clock, and turned back to Mum. "I found your precious clock under his bed, all wrapped up. He stole it." Father sneered, inching closer.

"No! It's not true. I got it back, and I was going to give it back to Mum." Magnus held the clock out in front of him.

Mum put her arm in front of Magnus. "Don't hurt him."

"A father needs to discipline his son when he doesn't listen." Father pushed past Mum and stepped toward Magnus.

Magnus' eyes were bright and defiant. "I'm not afraid of you."

"You should be." Father said, right before he slapped Magnus across the face, and knocked his glasses off and onto the floor.

"Leave him alone. Leave us alone!" Mum pulled Father back, and held his arms behind his back.

Magnus, unable to see without his glasses, and still clutching Big Ben, hurried to help Mum.

He didn't see the single ball of gray yarn that had rolled off the side table and onto the floor, when the caravan had shifted.

And he tripped.

As Magnus toppled forward, the Big Ben clock flew out of his hand, and barreled across the room toward Father.

Big Ben's *very* pointy and *very* sharp spire sunk deep into Father's bulging belly.

"Son of a…!" Father cried out in pain, cringing. He dropped to his knees, holding his stomach.

The Big Ben clock dropped to the floor with a thud, and then began to chime the Westminster Quarters.

As the clock chime rang out, everything, and everyone, was very still… Father was lying on the floor, Mum was leaned against the wall, and Magnus sat cross-legged next to the Christmas tree.

When the chiming stopped, Father raised his head, and slowly dragged himself over to the Christmas tree. "Say goodbye to your pressie." He snatched the beautifully wrapped present from underneath the tree, and held it up in the air. "Say goodbye, son."

Father got to his feet, and stumbled out of the caravan, slamming the door.

"Goodbye," Magnus sighed.

Magnus went to the window and watched as Father grabbed a can of kerosene, doused the present, and lit a match.

The present burst into flames.

Father staggered to the road, where the very same Bedford K dropside truck was parked out front, waiting. He climbed into the passenger side of the cab, and the truck's lights switched on.

Magnus watched as the truck pulled away.

Magnus moved to the side table, pulled a folded piece of paper from his pocket, and smoothed it flat.

It was Magnus' letter to Father Christmas.

Dear Father Christmas,
I have tried very hard to be good this year, although I must admit that I haven't have faltered occasionally. If you could find it in your hear heart to look past my failings, my greatest wish is that I would have a wonderful Christmas with my family. I really don't need any presents but if I'm honest it would be nice to have something to get open on Christmas day. If you have room in your sack I would appreciate a wristwatch as people often ask me the time. Hope you enjoy the holidays.
Sincerely,
Magnus

Magnus grabbed a pencil from a nearby table, and carefully crossed out several lines.

He closed his eyes for a moment, then lifted the pencil and began to write.

I wish

...

Outside the caravan, the present from Father had turned to cinders. The embers cracked and glowed.

Magnus hurried down the steps, and marched toward the fire, with his letter in hand.

Magnus crumpled the letter up into a ball and threw it onto the embers. The flames immediately licked, and then engulfed the paper.

He watched as the smoke ascended up into the night sky, and up to the vault of heaven.

Chapter 20

Mum stood in the darkened hallway, and gently knocked on the bedroom door.

"Magnus?"

Mum pushed the door open, and looked around Magnus' room. It was a cramped space the size of a closet, but everything was in its place. His clothes were folded and stacked neatly on a shelf, and his pale blue bedspread was pulled tight and neat.

Mum picked up a small pillow, embroidered with the letter "M," and traced the cursive with her finger. "Magnus."

She fluffed the pillow and placed it carefully at the head of the bed. "Magnus?"

Mum moved down the hallway and pushed the door open to the kitchen. "Magnus?" Her call was louder this time. She retreated back into the living area, and noticed the Big Ben clock, still lying on the floor. She picked it up, and set it carefully back on the table. "Where are you?"

Silence.

Mum moved to the door, and placed her hand on the metal frame. She stood there for a moment, and began to weep. "I can't." She sat down in front of the door, and covered her face with her hands.

> "When by my solitary hearth I sit,
> And hateful thoughts enwrap my soul in gloom;
> When no fair dreams before my "mind's eye" flit,
> And the bare heath of life presents no bloom;
> Sweet Hope, ethereal balm upon me shed,
> And wave they silver pinions o'er my head."

Mum took a deep breath, and then stood up.

Still in her dressing gown, Mum shrugged into a winter coat, and forced her bare feet into a small pair of wellington boots.

She opened the door, to gusting wind and pouring rain.

And for the first time in many years, she stepped outside.

…

Sudbury's sidewalks were bustling, as Mum scrambled through the streets, searching the faces of each and every child as they walked past.

The door chimed as Mum stepped inside the butcher shop. She glanced around the shop, and then up at the dozens of Christmas geese hanging from the ceiling.

"Can I help you?" The butcher asked, as he wiped down the counter.

"I'm looking for my son."

"Did you check the sweet shop?" The butcher winked. "That's where they usually find them."

"I thought he might have come here." Mum wrung her hands. "He's just ten, with flaxen hair and thick, black glasses that sit perched at the end of his little button nose." Mum smiled up at the butcher. "And he's got bright, blue eyes that are full of kindness, and... Hope."

"You mean Magnus."

Mum turned to see the angelic Abigail beaming up at her. "Yes, I'm his mum and I'm looking for him."

"I saw him."

"You did? When?" Mum asked, breathlessly.

"Earlier this afternoon."

Mum's face fell. "Oh... If you see him again, will you please tell him I'm looking for him?"

Abigail nodded. "I will."

...

As Mum pushed past the Christmas throngs, a group of carolers stood on the corner, singing.

Mum stopped, and watched as they swayed in unison. It was cold outside, but their faces were warm and bright.

And our eyes at last shall see Him,
Through His own redeeming love,
For that Child, so dear and gentle,
Is our Lord in Heaven above;
And He leads His children on,
To the place where He is gone.

"Out shopping I see." Mrs. Hurst stepped in front of Mum, blocking her view.

"No, I..."

"In case you're wondering, the doctor says Andy should regain full vision." Mrs. Hurst leaned in. "As a mother, I'm concerned for your boy, and his tendencies. I'm sure your husband learned a thing or two about discipline during his stint in the graybar hotel. Hopefully he can set the lad straight."

Mum was at a loss for words.

"You may also want to keep him away from the little dwarf he's been consorting with."

"Dwarf?"

"The dwarf that lives in the stately home at the top of the hill. He's been spoiled rotten, overindulged, and as a result has become quite an ill-mannered child."

"Enough." Mum shouted, her eyes wide. "Kindness is a virtue, Mrs. Hurst."

Mrs. Hurst closed her mouth.

"Merry Christmas," Mum said, before she turned and made her way through the crowd.

…

Mum hurried through the rain to the great and grand doors of Richard's stately home, and began pounding the lion's head knocker against its plate.

The very tall man opened the door, looking cross. "Good evening."

"I'm looking for my…"

"…I'm sorry, but we are not accepting visitors at this late hour."

He started to close the door, but Mum pushed it open. "My son! I'm looking for my son. He's a friend of the little boy that lives here."

"I'm afraid that Master McNaulty has retired for the evening, and cannot be of help."

Richard peeked out from behind the tall man. "Are you Magnus' mum?"

Mum glanced down at Richard. "I am." Mum crouched down to meet Richard's eye line. "He ran away earlier this evening. Do you know where I might find him?"

Richard shook his head. "I'm sorry. I don't."

Mum dropped to her knees, and wiped her teary eyes with the sleeve of her coat.

"When you find him, will you tell him that I'm very sorry?"

Mum nodded.

"And that I would very much like to be his friend again."

"I will." Mum rose to her feet, and began to back away from the door.

Richard stepped out in front of the tall man, and called after Mum, "He thought the pen was magical, but it wasn't. I wished to be taller and nothing happened."

Mum's eyes narrowed. "Magnus thought the pen from Agnus was magical?"

"And would you please tell him that I'm very, very sorry for binning it." Richard paused. "If I knew where all the rubbish ended up, I would go there and find it for him."

Chapter 21

Mum shivered against the bitter cold, as she clambered up the mountain of rubbish and rejectamenta. The evening sky was thick with falling snow.

"Magnus!" Mum pulled herself up to the top of the pile, and looked out across the landfill.

"Magnus!" She called again, but her words were swallowed up and muted by the snow flurries. She collapsed in a heap, and began weeping.

"Mum?"

Mum raised her head. "Magnus?"

Magnus quickly climbed over the mound of debris. "What are you doing here?"

"I came to find you." Mum said gently. "Your friend Richard told me about the pen."

133

"I need to find it."

Mum surveyed the landfill. "It's impossible. It's like finding a needle in a haystack."

Magnus stood firm. "I have to."

"Magnus, it's cold, and dark, and…"

"I have to find it!" Magnus ripped open a paper bag and emptied out the contents. He choked back tears as he watched the litter fall to the ground. "I need to write a different ending!"

"Magnus." Mum reached for Magnus' hand, but then stopped herself.

Magnus sat himself down on the pile of rubbish, and put his head in his hands. "He said he was just waiting for us to both leave so he could take our home."

Mum nodded. "Just like he took Agnus' caravan."

"And now that you've left the caravan…" Magnus shook his head. "I thought you would never leave."

Mum kneeled down next to Magnus. "I had to come find you."

Magnus looked up at Mum, his eyes wet with tears. "But now he's probably taken it… Our home."

Mum put her arm on Magnus' shoulder and pulled him close. "My sweet Magnus, home is wherever we are… Together."

…

Magnus and Mum sat side by side as the bus chugged along the road toward home. Magnus stared out of the window, and up into the night sky, where big, white flakes were softly falling.

"Magnus."

"Yes?" Magnus turned to Mum. She pushed the damp hair from Magnus' eyes, and kissed him gently on the forehead.

And I remember the day he was born. He had a full head of flaxen hair, and those bright, blue eyes.
Those eyes!
They were so full of life, and zest, and oomph.
O bright-eyed hope!

Magnus and Mum swayed as the double-decker turned the corner.

He is magnificent, isn't he?

To Hope.

Whene'er the fate of those I hold most dear
Tells to my fearful breast a tale of sorrow,
O bright-eyed Hope, my morbid fancy cheer;
Let me awhile thy sweetest comforts borrow:
Thy heaven-born radiance around me shed,
And wave thy silver pinions o'er my head!

And as, in sparkling majesty, a star
Gilds the bright summit of some gloomy cloud;
Brightening the half veil'd face of heaven afar:
So, when dark thoughts my boding spirit shroud,
Sweet Hope, celestial influence round me shed,
Waving thy silver pinions o'er my head.

- John Keats

The End

A NOTE TO READERS

This book is a work of fiction.

The names, places, and events in this book are completely fictional, and a product of the author's imagination. Any resemblance to actual persons, living or dead, or actual events, is coincidental.

...

This book is also a work of magic.

I don't know how this story fell out of my head and landed on the page, but it did.

About seven or eight years ago, I joined a writing group and we were tasked with writing a short story to share. There was no theme, or limitations, or genre: "Just write a story."

As I sat at my kitchen table, tapping my pen on the pad, staring out my window at the treetops, I was daunted by the freedom. I didn't want to show up the following Saturday without something to present (I'm a keener), so I sat and waited for inspiration to strike.

Full disclosure: Sometimes inspiration strikes, and sometimes I spend two hours shopping on Amazon.

I sipped my coffee (there's always coffee) and let my mind wander. And then, suddenly, my imagination opened up, and there he was… *Magnus*.

I could picture him in my head – the way he walked, the way he talked, the way he interacted with strangers, and the way his hair flopped down over his eyes. Yes, Magnus was a "teller of untruths," but he was so full of love, you couldn't help but love him too.

That Saturday I shared the first five pages of *Magnus the Magnificent.*

The following year I moved to England and took a screenwriting certificate program at Oxford. It was there I began work on the screenplay of *Magnus the Magnificent.*

I felt very inspired while living in England. I loved donning a pair of wellington boots and taking a long stroll through the countryside, rain or shine. I loved stopping in a pub to have a pint and warm my (always damp!) feet by the fire. I loved scouring the used bookshops in Oxford and discovering hand-written messages on the first page. Most of all, I loved eavesdropping, and occasionally striking up conversations with strangers. These little moments gave life to my writing, and helped shape the story of Magnus.

In England, ideas seemed to find me wherever I went… I had to keep a notebook with me at all times because the ideas were flowing like Texas crude (in the 80s, obviously not now, as we all know that the fossil fuel industry is going the way of the dinosaur, due to global capitalism's devastating overconsumption of our earth's natural resources).

I digress.

I don't understand *inspiration*, but I think Elizabeth Gilbert nailed it on the head in her book about creativity, titled, "Big Magic": "…Inspiration is still sitting there right beside me, and it is trying. Inspiration is trying to send me messages in every form it can – through dreams, through portents, through clues, through coincidences, through déjà vu, through kismet, through surprising waves of attraction and reaction, through the chills that run up my arms, through the hair that stands up on the back of my neck, through the pleasure of something new and surprising, through stubborn ideas that keep me awake all night long . . . whatever works. Inspiration is always trying to work with me."

Magnus *almost* seemed to write itself (in truth, it was definitely me sitting at a desk for hours on end).

When I finished *Magnus* in 2013, I entered it into the Academy's Nicholl Fellowship in Screenwriting Competition, and it advanced to become a Semifinalist (*ahem*, the top 146 scripts of 7,251 entries *cough*). It meant a lot that the Academy's readers connected with the story. While I have a real fondness for the screenplay, I have always wanted to share *Magnus* with a wider audience.

So, I went back to those first five pages written seven or eight years ago, and once again, sat down and waited for inspiration to strike (and obviously spent some time on Amazon).

And here we are.

I don't fully understand inspiration or how *Magnus* came to be, but I am grateful to live in a world filled with *big magic*.

- KM

ACKNOWLEDGMENTS

There are many people that helped with this book.

Some of them know that they were helpful, and some of them were helpful without even knowing it.

The Lloydster, *for everything*
The 'rents, *for raising me right*
Madeline, *for being you (and Magnus)*
Michelle, *for telling me not to quit*
My nearest and dearest, *for the love and encouragement*
Neff, *for being my editor and a pal*
Roald Dahl, *for the spark*
Sufjan Stevens, *for the tug on my heartstrings*

ABOUT THE AUTHOR

KIMBERLY MANKY is a Storyteller, Sparkplug and Ideas Machine from Northern Canada. Her hobbies include eating, drinking, laughing, and dreaming dreams. She lives in Canada with the Lloydster.

holdyourhorse.wordpress.com

Made in the USA
San Bernardino, CA
07 December 2016